ROLE PLAY

ROLE PLAY

Anne Melville

SEVERN SH HOUSE

This first world edition published in Great Britain 1996 by
SEVERN HOUSE PUBLISHERS LTD of
9–15 High Street, Sutton, Surrey SM1 1DF.
First published in the USA 1996 by
SEVERN HOUSE PUBLISHERS INC. of
595 Madison Avenue, New York, NY 10022.

British Library Cataloguing in Publication Data

Melville, Anne
     Role play
     1. English fiction – 20th century
     I. Title
     823.9′14 [F]

     ISBN 0-7278-5142-X

Typeset by Palimpsest Book Production Limited,
Polmont, Stirlingshire, Scotland.
Printed and bound in Great Britain by
Creative Print and Design, Ebbw Vale, Wales.

Chapter One

There was a storm in the night: a real humdinger of a summer storm which crashed and flashed overhead as though we were under bombardment. The sort of storm that, like a fractious child, keeps you awake till the small hours and then rouses you in the morning with a sunny smile. All over now. Another lovely day. It must have been while that storm was at its height that Rufus Fergie, on the other side of the world, pressed the SEND button to despatch the message which was to tip me into a cauldron of deceit, disappearance and death.

The fax machine was low on my list of priorities that morning. First job was to inspect the attics. Even what the weather people call a mild precipitation translates into a puddle once the water has cascaded down a steeply-pitched roof which is more than two hundred years old; and this had been real rain. My great-grandfather kept his servants on the top floor. I sometimes think that I could make my fortune by fish-farming up there.

The roof and I have been waging a running battle for years. I sneak up quietly, positioning yet another blue plastic bucket – twenty pence from the Cancer Research Charity Shop – to catch a leak which it thinks I haven't noticed. The next round, if the rain stops for long enough, involves me in trying not to tip a bucketful of a disgustingly black, adhesive and foul-smelling substance over myself while climbing through a trap door. Then, of course the roof goes off in a sulk to look for a new weak spot. A darkening becomes a dampness, a single drop of water swells and hangs without falling for a day or two; and suddenly it's drip, drip, drip, getting ready for whoosh.

On that morning in July, the roof was winning, and I felt pretty gloomy as I opened windows and started emptying out buckets. There was something wrong about the day: some small cloud just out of sight in that clear sky – but I wasn't exactly sure what it could be. Perhaps it was just that ancestral piety and gratitude for past generosity have to struggle for survival at six o'clock in the morning. My grandfather may have thought he was doing me a favour when he skipped over his only son and left his home directly to his granddaughter; but I wasn't entirely joking when I celebrated ownership at the age of twenty-one by re-christening the house. Once upon a time it was Headington Home Farm; but it's called The Millstone now.

Day-to-day expenses can be managed, with the help of my pupil-boarders. I'm a qualified teacher of English as a Foreign Language and I offer intensive month-long courses to six adult students at a time. Their fees cover normal household expenses, keep me up-to-date in sound and video equipment and even stretch to the alarming cost of veterinary treatment for a sick dog. But the price of a new roof for an eighteenth-century house is the sort of sum that keeps one awake at night, wondering how easy it would be to rob a bank. Oh well.

Last stop on my round was a room in the front of the house, with a bigger window than the others. I was able to send a bucketful of water curving through the air with a satisfying swish. From down below, two seconds later, came an aggrieved shout. "Oi!"

Christ! The postman never came that early. I leaned out

of the window and saw with dismay that the chap I had just soaked was Mort Goodison, our friendly neighbourhood policeman. Being neighbourhood means that he patrols Headington on a bicycle instead of in a helicopter. Being friendly means that he delivers confidential assessments of the degree of damage likely to be inflicted by visiting football fans when Oxford United play at home, and is willing to let my students practise on him even when it means answering the same question six times in a morning. Treating him like an alley cat was not the best way to repay past kindness. I hurled myself downstairs, ready to offer apologies and hot or strong drinks.

"Mort, I'm so sorry. I didn't look. Didn't expect anyone to be about at this hour. Come into the kitchen and take off everything that's wet."

"Ah, if only you meant it, Kit my love! I'm soaked to the skin."

"I meant it. The Aga will dry it all. I'll find something for you in the role-play cupboard."

What would be a dressing-up cupboard in normal households – households with a mother and two point three children – serves for role play in mine. All the students who come to me have already been learning English for several years and usually they can read and write it well. What most of them need is the ability to cope with life in Britain and to hold their own in every kind of conversation from casual chat to serious discussion.

One of the most effective ways of teaching them to express themselves clearly – and to extend their vocabularies at the same time – is through role play. I choose a setting – a job interview, for example, or a hospital casualty department – and give each member of the group a card. It tells her who she is and gives a background of relevant facts so that she can ask and answer questions confidently, adding embellishments as she chooses. Dressing up for the parts is only a bit of fun, not an essential, but it helps to banish shyness.

What role would Mort like to play, I wondered? An academic gown would not provide sufficient cover, and it might be wise to conceal the fact that I keep a complete policeman's outfit to hand: I'm not absolutely sure that it's legal. In the end I returned to the kitchen with a cosy jogger's two-piece and we sat at the big pine table with the first coffee of the day.

"I really am sorry, Mort. But you don't usually start so early, do you?"

"I wasn't starting, Kit my love: I was finishing. I've been down in the city all night, skulking round ladies' lavatories. I imagine you've read in the local paper about this rapist who's on the loose."

"Yes. He got a girl from one of the North Oxford language schools who'd missed the last bus."

"She was the fourth in three months," Mort said baldly.

"The paper didn't mention that. It ought to have, to put women on the alert."

"The paper didn't know. We didn't know. It was only when that last one, the Jap, got some publicity that the others started to speak up. Or else we heard from the school principals, who'd been told at the time but didn't want to frighten off future enrolments by letting word get round. The thing is, all the victims have been foreign girls. It can't be coincidence. The rapist must be going for them specially. Perhaps he hopes they'll be too frightened to go to the police – or that even if he gets caught, they'll be back in their own countries by the time the case comes to court, and won't come back to give evidence."

"So you've come to warn me to look after my girls. That's good of you, Mort. More coffee? And how about some of Maggie's gingerbread?"

4

"Great, thanks. But as for the warning, not exactly. I did wonder . . ." Mort isn't often lost for words, but he must have known he was on dangerous ground. "These girls you have here. They're more mature than most. Better able to look after themselves. And they operate as a group. I just wondered . . ."

The audacity of the suggestion almost took my breath away. "You're not suggesting that I should provide you with a tethered goat to trap a tiger!"

"Well, not exactly that. But if one of them was willing to help . . . There'd be no danger. The place would be swarming with police."

"Surely you use WPCs for this sort of thing."

"When I said 'foreign girls', perhaps I wasn't being specific enough. Asian girls is what he's going for: Chinese, Japanese, Vietnamese. And we haven't got any of those on the establishment."

"You must be out of your mind if you think I could provide you with rape bait!" The girls who come to me are sent by rich parents, or else by sponsors who've picked them for character as well as academic ability. They choose me rather than any of the big language schools because they know that my groups, besides being small, are either all-male or all-female and there's not going to be any hanky-panky. "I'm sorry, Mort, but I'm a teacher, not a detective."

"It was one of your groups which did us so well with that shoplifting gang."

"Only by accident."

That particular incident had, as a matter of fact, proved very satisfying. I'd sent one of my all-male groups down into Oxford to talk in pairs to shop customers as though they were doing a survey. They were instructed to move from shop to shop every hour, in order to make comparisons; and one pair had noticed some odd behaviour

5

repeated by the same people on different premises. They did everything right – alerted a store detective, kept an eye on the shoplifters and reported what they had seen in clear and confident English. One of the other four had even given chase and brought down a member of the gang who made a run for it. I was proud of them all – but that didn't mean that I was proposing to organise future classes as a posse of private investigators.

"Is that really why you came?" I asked curiously.

"No, my love. Just thought I'd try my luck while you were feeling guilty at giving me pneumonia. No, I came with a note about the next court hearing for that shoplifting case. Your lads will be needed to give evidence. Are they still in England?"

"Three of them are – including both the two who first noticed what was going on. Will that be enough?"

Sasha had come from St Petersburg, sponsored by a British firm which was trying to do business there. They'd first brought him over three years earlier for a two-month intermediate English course in Bournemouth. Now that he'd graduated in Russia, they reckoned that after extra coaching from me and a couple of months in their London office he'd be ready in October to tackle a degree course over here in business management. He was one of the brightest students I had ever taught. One of the most charming, as well – although sometimes when he was drunk there was a darkness in his eyes which was deeper than melancholy. Typically Russian, I suppose.

By contrast, Jian-li – the one who had sprinted after the shoplifter and wrestled him to the ground – was the dullest so-called advanced pupil I'd struggled with for a long time. He had a degree from Beijing Forestry University and had followed that – also in Beijing – with a special course in English for Academic Purposes, designed for students who were going on to higher degrees in Britain

6

or the United States. Presumably he was a high-flyer where trees were concerned, but whoever had certified his English as being up to advanced standard must have done the marking with his eyes shut.

In any other country I would have presumed that money had changed hands; but from friends working in China I had learned enough about local habits to guess at a likelier explanation. No doubt Jian-li's father had sufficient influence to block the promotion or arrange for the transfer of any examiner who refused to sign the vital certificate. That was none of my business. His reason for enrolling at The Millstone was to become at ease in ordinary English life and conversation, and that was what I'd tried my best to achieve for him.

The other witness, Andris Goonewardene, was older than these two: about thirty. He had already qualified as a doctor in Sri Lanka and had a provisional offer of a job in England, subject to registration. Doctors from overseas, unless they come from the European Community, find when they arrive here that their qualifications are viewed with deep suspicion. They're only given limited registration to start with, and before they're let loose on unsuspecting patients they have to jump the PLAB hurdle. Quite right too – although it's unfortunate that while the EC doctors tend to have white skins, most of the others turn out to be brown or black.

The Professional and Linguistic Assessment is a tough test of both medical knowledge and proficiency in English, but it hadn't seemed to me that Andris would have much trouble. I couldn't judge how good he was at medicine, but his English was fluent. All he had wanted from my course, probably, was confidence. In our role play sessions he'd usually been allowed to play himself, a doctor, while the others acted as accident victims or took pleasure – with a little help from me – in trying to catch him out with all the extraordinary euphemisms which the British apply to micturition and pregnancy.

I promised to line them all up for the hearing and allowed Mort to cycle off in the jogging suit with his uniform in a shopping bag. I was just washing up the coffee cups when Maggie arrived in the kitchen.

Maggie is a sort of aunt, in that my grandparents adopted her when she was fourteen. She was born profoundly deaf. If someone had taken her in hand right from the start, I imagine that she could have been taught to speak. But nobody did, so she is mute as well as deaf. If someone had sent her to a special school she would presumably have received some sort of education, but nobody did that either. Instead, I suppose she sat in the back row of a classroom for nine years, cocooned in her own silence, understanding nothing and coming to life only when she was allowed to paint or sew. By the time her mother died and she came to my grandfather's attention, she was certainly illiterate and was assumed to be mentally deficient.

Grandfather was a surgeon, and was sorry for the child; but there was nothing he could do for her hearing. He was impressed, though, by the cleanness and neatness of her appearance, the skill with which she embroidered and the quickness with which she absorbed any lesson which could be passed on purely by practical demonstration. He took her into his household and arranged for her to be taught language, gardening and cookery.

Language must have been a struggle. Even an illiterate has heard words spoken and knows what they mean, but Maggie would have had no concept of the names of objects or actions at all. Even now, forty-odd years later, communication is best kept basic. Gardening was not a success. She has always been nervous of open spaces in which she is unable to hear danger

8

approaching. But she proved to have a natural talent for cooking and housekeeping and took over the running of The Millstone when she was only seventeen, after my grandmother died.

The house is her life. When I inherited it, it was clear that Maggie went with the property. Maggie is the reason why I was never able to do what all young TEFL teachers plan and long to do – to explore the world for ten years or so: a year here, a year there, working my way by teaching. I am better qualified now than any of my fellow-students on the course which earned us our first certificate, and I am probably a better teacher: but I am stuck, stuck, stuck in England. Maggie knows that. She knows that she, and not the house, is my millstone.

Gratitude overwhelms her. With the help of a single daily, she pays for my sacrifice by keeping this large, damp, decaying house as clean as in the days when it supported an army of servants. She cooks such delicious meals that I can justifiably charge hotel prices to my pupils. And her smile spreads a silent sunshine which is infectious: if you can't talk to someone, you *have* to smile.

Gratitude is an emotion I can't deal with, except by making myself grateful to her in return. On the notepad tied to her waist or the screen of the word machine kept in the kitchen I tell her over and over again how much I value the comforting arm with which she cuddles some homesick eighteen-year-old.

Three times a week I drive her and one of the students into Oxford to go shopping. The expedition, in this form, is not strictly necessary. I could do the marketing on my own, Maggie herself could cope with a supermarket without speaking, and even in Oxford's Covered Market everyone knows her and would fill a written order. But there is a particular value to students in reading out the list on her behalf, and answering questions if there is a problem. They are not playing a role now, but speaking words that need to be spoken. Shyness and hesitancy disappear. I have explained this to Maggie as well, and she is delighted to be useful.

On the morning after the storm she greeted me with her usual wave of the hand and then looked round the kitchen and asked a question, using the shorthand sign language which is personal to the two of us.

"Where's Griselda?"

The question wiped the smile from my face. That was what was wrong with the morning; the cloud in the sky. That was why I had emptied a bucket full of water over Mort. I had felt sure that there couldn't be anyone near the front door, because Griselda wasn't barking.

Griselda was Maggie's dog, specially trained to warn her of danger or visitors. There was never a closed door between the two of them. Maggie couldn't hear the barking, but Griselda had been trained to touch her leg with a paw, drawing attention to herself, before leading the way towards whatever had disturbed her.

She was our watchdog, although too old and gentle to act as a guard. Anyone who came near the house, whether by invitation or with criminal intent, would be announced not by a butler or an alarm system but by an elderly spaniel. But this morning Griselda hadn't barked.

Perhaps the storm had frightened her into silence. I dismissed this idea even before beginning to search the house. It wasn't too hard to guess what had happened. She was an old lady, and she had been ill for six weeks already.

I found her body in the office, lying near the fax

machine. Its gentle warble and flashing light must have been the last things to attract her attention; I could see that a message had come through during the night.

There was no time to consider it now, for Maggie had followed me in. We turned into each other's arms. The tears rolled silently down her cheeks and her chin jerked upwards as she tried to sniff them away. I would have liked to cry as well, but there were practical things to be done. Luckily it was my empty week – I reckon to keep a few days free between each course. I cuddled Maggie back into the kitchen and made her a cup of tea before moving Griselda's body.

This was not the occasion to be sentimental and argue that such a beloved member of the family could never be replaced. We needed a watch dog; and not just for Maggie's sake.

The Millstone is an unusually isolated house to find inside the boundaries of the City of Oxford. In its early days, as the Home Farm, it had a considerable acreage: but then the ring road came.

The ring road is one reason why I shall never be able to make my fortune by selling the house. Although the slope of the hill and a screen of trees keep the traffic out of sight, there is a perpetual rumble as cars speed between London and Cheltenham or Wales. I'm used to the noise by now, but anyone proposing to buy a mansion in which to live in style would look elsewhere.

The road itself swallowed a large chunk of the Home Farm's land. It's a dual carriageway, with an additional double cycle track on one side. There are wide grass verges and hedges, and the central reservation has also been allowed a generous space, laid out with grass and shrubs. This provides a necessary pausing place for anyone trying to cross the road – a rash endeavour, since this section of the ring road seems to double as a race track.

All the farmland on the far side of the road was sold as soon as it was cut off from the rest; there is a housing estate there now. But the family was able to keep more than just the spacious garden surrounding the house, complete with terraces and tennis court. There is a walled garden at a little distance, in which we grow vegetables. There are two orchards. And there is a considerable standing of what is not so much woodland as ancient forest. Beeches and copper beeches, oaks and hornbeams, limes and grey poplars and chestnuts – all huge and so old as to be dangerous, shedding branches without warning in gales. I love them all; but the darkness through which the approach drive meanders is so intense that the house is moated by it. If anything unpleasant were to happen at The Millstone, it could be a very long time before anyone noticed. I'm not a nervous type, but I sleep more soundly when I know that someone with an insistent bark is listening out for prowlers on my behalf.

Guessing that Griselda had not long to live, I had some weeks earlier put Maggie's name on the waiting list for a trained replacement. As soon as the charity opened for business, I rang to say that our case was now urgent. Only then did I remember that there was a fax waiting to be read. I ripped off the pages and sat down, feeling as though I'd already done a full day's work in the past three hours.

The first sheet was almost entirely white. The printed address, in both Japanese and Western script, was of an apartment in Tokyo. First of all came the heading, *STRICTLY PRIVATE AND CONFIDENTIAL:* underlined three times. Beneath that was a formal identification:

12

'From: Rufus Fergie.
To: Katherine Quilter.'

There was nothing else on the page but a huge diagonal scrawl:

'Hi, Kit! Remember me?'

The second page was covered with lines of Rufus's almost illegible handwriting, but it was a moment or two before I was ready to start reading it. Instead, my eyes turned first to the photograph which I still kept in the office. Heaven knows why I'd hung on to it. It was a happy photograph, but the happiness hadn't lasted long.

The photograph showed a man and two girls; all twenty-one years old. Rufus was the man in the middle: tall – very tall – blond and handsome. I was the beanpole on the left, with my eyebrows arching upwards to hit the bottom of my fringe. People are always accusing me of looking quizzical, whatever that may mean, but that's just the way my eyebrows were born. On the right of the photograph was Tilda, petite and sexy. Gamine hairstyle, tilt-up nose, dimpled cheeks, peachy complexion, perfect figure: a dish. At the moment when the shutter opened she was clinging on to Rufus and Rufus was clinging on to me: it made me feel good at the time.

The photograph was taken on the day we finished our TEFL certificate course. We'd all got jobs lined up. I was going off to Mexico, Tilda to Spain and Rufus to Libya. We both thought he was mad, but the money was good and the Foreign Office said cautiously that they couldn't see any objection. We knew we shouldn't see each other for a year, but that was the TEFL life. At the moment when the camera clicked there was still a week to go before my grandfather died and before I realised that that wasn't going to be *my* sort of TEFL life.

Both Tilda and I were head over heels in love with Rufus. We'd all been at university together before starting the course. He was my first lover – although not Tilda's – and I was such an old-fashioned girl that I thought this would give me some kind of claim on him; but Tilda was the one he chose. They got engaged the day before he left for Tripoli.

Not many people in our circle were as formal as that. Perhaps Rufus thought it was the only way to make sure that she would be waiting when he came back. The news of the engagement hurt at the time, hurt a lot – and the way Tilda behaved later hurt even more, because I liked to think that I would have shown more loyalty if Rufus had picked me; but I got over it. It was even possible to stay sort-of friends with Tilda. I wasn't always sure that I liked her, but we'd shared the happiest years of our lives, and that made a kind of bond. Perhaps, too, keeping in touch with her gave me a tenuous contact with the kind of career which might have been mine if it hadn't been for Maggie.

Tilda and I didn't actually see much of each other, because she was always abroad and I was always here, but I let her make a nest for herself in our old coach-house. Somewhere she could keep her things and rest for a day or two between jobs and visits. Rufus, though, I hadn't met for eight years, and had seen him only for a few seconds, three years back, when his face stared out of my television screen after the Libyans finally set him free.

I wasn't sure now that I wanted to get involved again. According to Tilda, the years of imprisonment – without trial and without knowing how long the ordeal would last – had knocked him off balance. Spooky was her word for it – but why should I believe Tilda, whose conscience could hardly have been clear? In any case, those quizzical eyebrows of mine don't exaggerate when they suggest insatiable curiosity. Of course I had to read the second page.

'I have some business to put your way,' wrote Rufus. 'Tilda told me, before she skipped, about the high-level operation you run. In particular, that when you teach girls, you don't have any boys on the premises. Is that still true? If so, there's someone for whom you could do a good turn.

She's a Japanese girl, orphaned, eighteen years old. Since her family is one of the richest and best-known in Japan, I'm not going to write her name here, because secrecy is important. She's probably known all her life that with such a fortune at stake, she was bound to be pushed into an arranged marriage, but she's only recently realised just how high her uncle and grandfather have set their sights. She may be too late to pick the juiciest plum on the tree; but this won't fall far short. She finds it frightening: who wouldn't? But she's used to doing what she's told.

This is where you come in. Her education has been carefully geared to her future life for several years already. Etiquette and languages are her most important subjects, and she can read and write English extremely well. (Nothing to do with me, that. I only know her because I visit her uncle's house, where she lives, to coach her cousin.) But like so many Japanese, she's desperately shy when it comes to speaking the language. Even her uncle, who can hardly bear to let her leave the house, realises that she's got to snap out of this and start gabbling. So she's to be let out of the cage for a month, as long as there's an equally safe (i.e. man-free) haven waiting to welcome her.

15

What do you reckon? Making sure that she's suitably chaperoned might be a bit of a nuisance, but you could charge anything you like. And think of the boost that it would give to your reputation in Japan. This is a family that wants nothing but the best. If you do a good job, you'll be the tops, and you'll have to put up crush barriers to hold back the rush.

Give me a ring and we'll talk about it.

All the best.

Rufus.'

I didn't need long to consider. Rufus hadn't spelled it out in so many words – and I had more reason than most people to know that his thoughts were as difficult to read as his handwriting – so I might have misunderstood. But it did seem to me that nothing but good could come from being able to claim a future member of the Japanese imperial family as an Old Girl.

It was the biggest mistake of my life.

Chapter Two

All my pupils and friends are warned that every incoming phone call to The Millstone will be recorded, whether it goes on the answerphone or is taken live. This is partly for Maggie's benefit, but also it's because of the system I operate with the students. They take it in turn to answer the phone and deal with the calls. It helps them to cope with difficult accents and unexpected topics – I have half a dozen jolly pals who delight in giving complicated messages in impenetrable Scots or Geordie voices. But just in case some vital piece of information fails to get through the system, I listen to all the recordings once a day.

For the phone call which came through five days after the storm, though, I was ready and waiting.

"Kit? Rufus here. I'm at Heathrow, and I've just handed Mayuko over to the Japanese ambassador."

"I thought you were going to bring her straight here."

"Protocol has decreed otherwise. Word has apparently gone out to the effect that she is to be treated as a national treasure. All the poor girl wants to do is to sleep, but she's been taken off for lunch. She'll be delivered to you at five."

"I'm sorry. I was looking forward to seeing you again."

"Me too. I'll try and drop in sometime in the next month. I thought I might nip over to Paris for a day or

17

two, but after that I'm planning a general swan round the south of England, looking up relatives and getting to know the old country again. Oh, just one thing I forgot to mention before, about Mayuko. No photographs, please. I gather that in England these days you can't trust anyone not to sell pictures to the press. I think that's everything. 'Bye for now."

Was I really disappointed at not seeing him, or rather relieved? Difficult to tell, so I didn't bother to work it out. Instead I rang my mother.

The arrangement that Mayuko should come to study with me had been made with extraordinary speed. I'd expected her to turn up in three months or so, rather than in a few days. According to Rufus, it was all part of an anti-kidnap strategy. Move secretly, move unexpectedly, move fast. Fear of kidnapping is hardly a normal part of my daily life, so I merely blinked and supposed they knew what they were doing. The snag was that I already had my next six students lined up, and thanks to the leaking roof there were no more bedrooms available in the house. I did consider commandeering Tilda's pied-a-terre in the coach-house, but July was the month when she was most likely to need it herself.

There was no way in which I was going to evict any of the six girls already booked, who had been given a detailed prospectus of the accommodation they could expect. But Rufus's mention of a chaperone had produced a perfect solution. Mayuko would sleep with my mother.

Mum lives in a small house in North Oxford while Dad lords it in the Master's Lodgings of a Cambridge college – and Lodgings, in this context, does not mean digs. The contrast is considerable; but her home is warm and comfortable and, although a good many years have passed since the divorce, she was still a lawfully wedded wife when he got his K. So it was Lady Quilter whom I was able to propose for the provision of bed and breakfast, escort service whenever required, and extra one-to-one English conversation.

My usual custom is to send an advance questionnaire to all prospective pupils, so that by the time they arrive I know what their particular needs are and can work out an individual study plan. But there hadn't been time to do that in Mayuko's case. Instead, it had been arranged that she should arrive the day before the other girls, so that I could give full attention to settling her in and drawing up a timetable. I had time for a chat with Mum after telling her what time to expect her lodger.

"I hope you're asking for a certificate, Kitten," she said. I could do without being called Kitten, but it's not easy to break the habit of twenty-nine years. We have a pact to the effect that she won't use the word if anyone else is listening.

"A certificate of competency in English, do you mean?"

"I mean nothing of the kind. A certificate of undamaged goods. Sounds to me as though in four weeks' time you'll be required to hand back one *virgo intacta*. You need to know what you're receiving."

"Oh really, Mum!" Daughters rarely concede that their mothers may be talking sense, and I still had no idea of the complications to come.

The process of discovery began at five o'clock precisely, when the doorbell rang.

Mayuko's appearance came as a surprise. It made sense that for a long plane journey she should wear a comfortable trouser suit and leave her long black hair to hang straight down her back. What had I expected – that she would turn up in kimono and obi, with her long black hair elaborately coiled into a chignon? Of course not. But what was unexpected was her lack of –

19

what was it? Personality? Poise? The aura of wealth? It had seemed a reasonable assumption that such a rich girl would be sophisticated, or at the very least self-possessed. She must, after all, have needed a certain amount of initiative and determination to get herself out of Japan. Instead, she looked desperately shy and nervous as she stood on the doorstep, staring down at her shoes. Rufus had warned me that she lacked confidence in speaking the language – which was usual enough – but this anxiety clearly went deeper than that.

Well, not surprising, perhaps, if she'd never lived anywhere but in her uncle's house and now found herself amongst foreigners in a country where everything must seem strange. I gave her my warmest smile and she bowed in greeting. Straight into Lesson One: the holding out of a hand to remind her that she had to shake it.

"How do you do, Mayuko?"

"How do you do." The words were whispered; hardly audible. But she raised her head to speak, and I was relieved to see that her dark eyes were alert and intelligent.

"Come along in, and welcome to England and to The Millstone." I gave a nod of thanks and dismissal to the chap standing beside her, assuming him to be the chauffeur, but he followed us in.

"Mr Tanaka from the embassy." Again, the words were hardly articulated as she performed the introduction.

"Please show me the house," he said, with no nonsense about greeting or handshaking. A bit put out, I had to remind myself that this was an unusual pupil, and led the way round the ground floor.

The drawing and dining rooms still serve their original purposes; but the morning room has become my private office. Each pupil has two individual tutorials a week with me there, but all the group activity goes on in the library and billiards room.

In the oak bookcases which line the library, bright editions of English fiction, ancient and modern, cheer up the sombre rows of my grandfather's medical books. Except for the classes and discussions which take place there in the mornings, this is a quiet room. There are six desks and upright chairs, six armchairs, and a display of magazines and daily papers.

The billiards room, by contrast, is full of gadgetry and for most of the time buzzes with activity. It looks a mess, but everything is useful. One end of the room is equipped for self-access work. There are cubicles with headphones and tape recorders and cassette machines for audio work, and a computer for word-processing and language games. In the larger section of the room I keep a video camera for recording role play sessions and a large television screen for playing back the tapes.

As well as the cupboard full of costumes, the room contains a variety of props to transform it into a shop, a railway station, a court of law. All this helps to banish self-consciousness. "We are only acting," the students say to themselves, and so they don't worry if they make mistakes while struggling to express some ambitious thought.

Mr Tanaka, acting the part of the inscrutable Oriental, revealed no admiration of all this equipment: he was only interested in the security of the windows. Since any kind of burglar alarm activated by movement or body heat would be in constant activity from homesick pupils wandering down at midnight to raid the larder, I had spent the money instead on special bolts and hinge locks; so I reckoned that The Millstone would pass with flying colours. That didn't prevent me from feeling indignant at the inspection, and

21

when he showed signs of moving upstairs I shook my head.

"I'll look after Mayuko from now on," I told him. "Thank you for bringing her. Goodbye."

As I moved him out of the house while shaking hands, Mayuko gave the first sign of animation since her arrival, pursing her lips as though she was tempted to smile but unsure whether she should. I smiled back.

"Would you like some tea, Mayuko?"

She nodded.

"I only respond to words. You have to tell me, 'Yes, please, Kit,' or, 'No, thank you, Kit'."

"Yes, please, Kit." Pronouncing my Christian name was an effort: she would clearly have liked greater formality, to show respect.

"Let's go into the kitchen, then." Before we moved, I explained about Maggie, watching Mayuko's eyes to check that she could understand me. Maggie was already smiling as she waited to be introduced, and pointed to a row of labelled tea containers, inviting a choice. Mayuko also pointed.

"Which one have you chosen?" I asked.

Again the answer came in a whisper, which I pretended not to hear.

"You'll have to speak more clearly for me. My hearing's not too good."

Recognising this for the untruth it was, Mayuko gave her half-smile again. "Fujian Oolong."

"Good." This particular tea had been a present from Jian-li, my most recent Chinese pupil. It tasted like an insipid variety of senna pods and had only survived immediate despatch to the dustbin because Jian-li himself was likely to call in again when he returned to Oxford for the shoplifting trial.

Over three pots of tea – since I drink weak Earl Grey

22

and Maggie likes the sort of dark brown tannic acid that a spoon will stand up in – I chatted to Mayuko about her journey. I was testing her and she showed by her amusement that she knew it. The result was encouraging. Her understanding of English was excellent, and she rarely had to search for a word or form of speech in reply, although the habit of lowering her head and whispering was obviously engrained. It looked as though all she needed me to teach her was confidence.

I spent half an hour discussing her timetable for the coming month with her and then, at six o'clock, drove her to North Oxford. She was tired after the flight and wanted nothing more to eat after the embassy lunch. Mum gave her a warm welcome while I added a few words of warning on the subject of baths. Every nationality has some little habit which is taken for granted at home but can cause a British hostess to go up in smoke, and flooding the bathroom ranks high on the list of potential disaster areas. By seven o'clock she had retired to bed.

I fancied an early night myself. The other six girls were all due to arrive the next morning; and acting as hotel manager as well as teacher makes reception day a strain. Besides, once the four-week course starts I reckon to work an eighteen-hour day, so it's as well to start fresh.

Rufus phoned just as I was about to get into a bath.

"Kit. Rufus here. All well? Mayuko arrived safely?"

"Yes, fine. She seems a nice girl. Desperately shy, though, as you warned me."

"She was pretty scared on the plane. She's never been out of the country before. I had to keep reassuring her that people would be friendly. And of course she's had the family's expectations so firmly drummed into her that maybe she sees this as a test: if she can't cope, her whole future might disappear. But I have absolute faith in your ability to make her feel at home and happy. And who

23

knows, one of these days some great question of foreign policy may be influenced by the impression that this one girl gets from her stay in England."

My arched eyebrows disappeared into my fringe. Not because of the foreign policy bit. I've always recognised that some really minor experience – good or bad – can influence for life a bright student who goes on to become important in his own country. No, what amused me was Rufus's assumption that he knew what kind of a person I was. But he was still talking.

"Could you let me have your mother's phone number? So that I can give Mayuko a ring and chat to her if she's feeling homesick."

I gave him the number, but told him not to call that evening. "She'll be asleep now. And if you do talk to her, Rufus, you're not to let her speak Japanese."

I go to a lot of trouble to make sure that no two pupils in any group speak the same language. Total immersion in English is the name of the game, and I didn't want Rufus providing temptation.

"Yes, ma'am. Anything you say, ma'am."

"Have you got a phone number for yourself, Rufus? Just in case."

"Not at the moment. I'm on the move. But I'll keep in touch. 'Bye for now."

After he rang off I sat for a moment on the bed, naked except for a wrist-watch, thinking about Rufus. His voice had changed between midday and evening. In this second call it had been high-pitched, excited. That note of excitement had been familiar to me once. Who was the lucky lady tonight, I wondered. Except that perhaps she wasn't so lucky. Even as a carefree undergraduate, laying on the charm, Rufus had been unreliable; and if Tilda was to be believed, he had lost the charm while preserving the unreliability.

24

Not surprising, perhaps, in the light of his experience in Libya. What had happened to Rufus there was this:

At the end of his year's teaching in Tripoli he was driving himself to the airport when a small boy, chasing a ball, ran into the side of the car. Not in front of it; into the side. But his head was down and he wasn't looking and he died. Rufus was automatically arrested and put into prison. The system was that the parents of the dead child had the right to decide on a suitable punishment, and once they'd got over the first grief, they agreed (for a financial consideration) that it was their son's own fault. But that took three months, and in the meantime Colonel Gaddafi had become seriously displeased with Britain and the United States. The frontiers were closed and the prison doors stayed locked.

Five years passed before there was a break in the diplomatic clouds. Or perhaps it was just that the West had something or somebody valuable to exchange. It must have been a condition of the release that there should be no fuss. On television there was a single glimpse of Rufus arriving at Heathrow, and then silence. None of the excitement which followed the return of the hostages from Beirut. No press conferences, no periods of rehabilitation.

What happened next I know only from Tilda. On his return to England Rufus had one blazing row with the Foreign Office, whom he blamed for not doing enough – or, indeed, anything at all – to get him out; and a second blazing row with the British part-owners of the school in Tripoli, who had felt no obligation to go on paying his salary after the expiry of the one-year contract. His mother had died while he was in prison, so there was nothing to keep him in England, and his only ambition was to shake the dust of his native country off his feet for ever.

Tilda was teaching on a summer course on the south coast at the time, as many TEFL teachers do between overseas jobs. Five years earlier she'd been completely devastated when Rufus never arrived at Heathrow on the flight from Tripoli; and for a year after that she'd done her best to press for some kind of diplomatic negotiations. But she had a living to earn and her work took her abroad, and as she wasn't an experienced publicist, I think she was swamped by a feeling of hopelessness. She gave up, reconciling herself to the fact that Rufus would be fed up with her for not trying harder. After all, it must have been tough for someone who was pretty and vivacious and twenty-three years old to condemn herself to an unlimited period of mourning and chastity. All the same, I like to think – but there's no point in going into that now.

Anyway, when Rufus swooped down on Tilda in Bournemouth, told her that he'd got a permanent job in Japan and asked her to come with him, it must have seemed the only decent thing to do. She lasted less than three months in Tokyo, and it was made very clear to me when she arrived unexpectedly back at the coach-house, looking pale and ill, that questions would not be welcome. I never found out what had happened.

All this didn't take as long to remember as it has to write down; but it was too long. What I should have been remembering was that the bath was running. I was catching Japanese bad habits.

An hour later, when I'd mopped up most of the mess and carried the bathroom carpet down to the boiler room and, at last, had my bath, I collapsed into bed and went straight to sleep – until the telephone awakened me at two in the morning.

Swearing under my breath, I turned on the light. This sort of thing happens to me quite often. Ex-pupils and old friends from the TEFL world are scattered all over the globe, and not all of them stop to work out what time it is in England before settling down to a comfortable chat. But today the call came from nearer home.

"Kitten?" It was Mum speaking, in the same sort of whisper which Mayuko had adopted earlier in the day. "Sorry to wake you, darling. But I need your advice. We've got a prowler."

I sat up, alarmed. "Inside the house?"

"No. In the garden. I actually saw him climb over the wall. I've been down to check that all the windows and doors are locked, and in fact he doesn't seem to be moving. But I know he's there. I could have simply phoned for the police to come, of course. But you specially said that there must be no publicity about Mayuko being in England, so I thought I'd better ask you first."

"I'll come over myself." At that time of night it would only take ten minutes. "Stay where you can see if he moves, Mum. And keep the telephone in your hand. If you hear any sound of him trying to break in, call the police without waiting for me. But I won't be long."

I dashed down to the role play cupboard before getting dressed. Impersonating a police officer in a public place is an offence, but a burglar was hardly likely to report me. While I was about it I picked up an imitation gun and a real pair of handcuffs; there would be a torch in the car.

North Oxford is mainly covered with huge villas built for late-Victorian families with six children and as many servants. Most of them are converted into flats now, and the streets are permanently clogged with parked cars. But Mum had managed to get hold of one of a group of small modern houses, overlooking a tennis club and the Dragon School playing fields. Only a few yards past her front door the road comes to a full stop against the walls of Lady Margaret Hall, so even by day there's very little traffic movement and at night the silence is of the grave. I double-parked a short distance away and climbed quietly over a brick wall: not directly into Mum's own back garden but into the one next door.

The prowler was keeping as still as I was, so it took me a little while to adjust to the darkness and pick him out. He was looking towards the house, with his back to me. I climbed cautiously on to the flat roof of Mrs Mallory's shed, steadied my balance, and jumped.

"You're under arrest!" I shouted in the voice which I use for male parts in the role play sessions; and at the same time I shone the powerful torch straight into his eyes. This was intended to blind him, but had the secondary effect of revealing the face of a broken-nosed thug. He had so obviously been a boxer that I expected any resistance to come from his fists and didn't immediately see his foot kicking up towards my chin. Just in time, I got an arm across to guard it, but the force of the blow made me drop the torch, which lay on the ground, pointing uselessly at Mum's Busy Lizzies.

So it was war. I knew enough karate and judo not merely to defend myself but to go on the attack. More to the point, I knew the geography of the garden. The fight ended when I threw him back on to the sharp corner of the lead jardinière filled with geraniums. He let out one squawk of pain and another of fury as he felt the handcuffs click over his wrists.

An upstairs window opened in the next-door house and Mrs Mallory's pained voice floated down.

"Will you kindly be quiet! Some of us are trying to sleep." Anyone could get murdered in Heyford Close and if she was inconsiderate enough to scream during the process she could expect a note through the door next morning asking her to die more silently: it was that kind of a community.

Mum's own French windows slid open as, armed with

28

a tennis racquet, she came out to join in the fight. She had been sensible in keeping the doors locked till I came, but she is no little old lady, cowering in terror at every creak. Much of her time is spent as a volunteer worker in Oxfam's bookshop, but she also acts as coach at the tennis club across the road. She may be fifty, but she's as tall and thin and fit as I am; and just as willing to have a go.

I hustled the thug inside and turned on the light, allowing him a moment to puzzle over the relationship between a policeman's uniform and my long, straight, sleep-tousled hair.

"What the bloody hell's going on?" he spluttered. "Is it you I'm supposed to be guarding?"

"You tell me. And your story had better be good."

"I was hired as a guard, young lady. Dusk till dawn – well, till she's delivered up to some house in Headington."

"Who hired you?"

"Chap called Tanaka. Look, I've got an authority. Take the bloody cuffs off and I'll show you."

I found the paper before setting his hands free. He wasn't likely to have invented the name Tanaka. I rubbed my unnecessarily bruised arm.

"You've no right to lurk on private ground."

"I wasn't doing any damage."

"Next time you can explain that to the real police. Get out of here now, and tell your employer to phone me between nine and ten tomorrow morning. I'm not going to put up with this sort of thing."

Mum let him out of the house and returned with ice cubes to press on the bruise. Mayuko, in the front room, was presumably sleeping the sleep of the jet-lagged.

"I'm most impressed," Mum said. "Where did you learn to throw people about like that?"

"I did a course in self-defence for women once. And

29

I'm always learning new tricks in my pupil-lesson periods. There are a surprising number of judoists amongst the students."

Pupil-lessons are short periods when the students, one each day, teach instead of learning. They are, of course, practising their English all the time, and are expected to be particularly precise in order to make the subject clear. But the subjects are their own, and enthusiasm promotes fluency.

In my last group, for example, Andris had taught us all how to help people injured in road accidents. Sasha had helped me to put my accounts on computer, while the others watched and commented. Jian-li had made some really quite sensible suggestions about the care of my oldest trees, although he did so in such painful telegrammatic English that I still wondered how he'd ever earned his grant to come here. And Yilmaz, a Turk, had improved on the judo which earlier pupils had taught me by introducing some wrestling variations to confuse an opponent expecting an orthodox defence and counter-attack.

Afterwards, he and Jian-li had given an exhibition bout for the rest of us, with Yilmaz playing the part of a mugger's victim who intended to turn the tables. Each of the two had been so determined not to lose face by conceding defeat that I'd become quite worried at one point, and had to remind them that a demonstration didn't require a winner and a loser.

My pupils enjoy teaching – although as a rule they choose less aggressive subjects – and I like learning. I'd certainly learned a lot from Yilmaz; but I'd never expected to put what he taught me to such good use.

"I'm sorry about this, Mum," I said. "The impression I had to start with was that she had to be chaperoned just to protect her from unsuitable boyfriends." Nobody had mentioned the word kidnap until I commented on the speed with which the visit was arranged. "I shouldn't have asked you . . ."

"Don't worry about it, Kitten," Mum said comfortably. "Took me by surprise, that's all. As long as we know, it will be quite all right. There can't really be any danger of kidnapping, surely. They fixed it up so quickly, and nobody knows she's here."

"There's the ambassador and anyone he invited to lunch." I was uneasily aware that I didn't know anything about Japanese domestic politics. Suppose another powerful family had its own candidate for the imperial marriage, or whatever it was. But no, that was moving from speculation into fantasy. What I needed was a few hours of calming sleep.

"I shouldn't have disturbed you," she said. "Now that I'm in the picture, I can manage. The important thing is obviously that I should stick to her like glue whenever she isn't with you. I'll bring her up in time for lunch tomorrow; or rather today. And I shall want a receipt."

We both grinned as we kissed good-night. I drove home carefully, neither too fast nor too slowly, not wishing to be stopped in my police uniform. Mayuko's visit had not got off to the best of starts. But in a few hours' time the course proper would begin: intensive, carefully planned and allowing for very little unorganised time. I would tell Mr Tanaka to leave us alone, and from then on – I fondly hoped – everything would run smoothly.

Chapter Three

Ten days into the new course Mort called in to tell me that the Oxford rapist had struck again.

"Nasty one this time. Jumped a girl from behind. She seems to have put up more of a fight than the others, and he pretty near strangled her before she passed out. Lucky to be alive, it sounds."

"Was she able to describe him?"

"Only his hands and arms. Fair skin, fair hair, freckles. Not much to go on. You look after your young ladies now, Kit my love, especially if you've got any from the Far East."

I thanked him for the warning, but there was only Mayuko and she was never left alone. On the morning after the prowler incident I'd had a showdown over the phone with Mr Tanaka. But he explained that it was Mayuko's uncle who had ordered him to hire a guard. News of the rapist had apparently reached Tokyo when a Japanese girl became one of the victims.

It was easy to tell, as Tanaka set out to calm me down, that he was glad to feel that the embassy need not be responsible for Mayuko's safety. If I wished to alter the arangement with the bodyguard, that would be a matter for me to discuss directly with Uncle Shin. In short, he was a thoroughly diplomatic diplomat and merely wanted to make it clear that if anything went wrong it would be nothing to do with him.

The prospect of a telephone conversation with a tyrannical Uncle Shin, who might well not speak English, was not inviting. The matter was settled on the basis that, now that I knew what was going on, I would raise no objection to letting the thug hang around Heyford Close, as long as he didn't trespass on private property or disturb the neighbours. So that was agreed, and I could concentrate on my teaching.

On this month's course there was a Finnish ex-teacher of Russian who had discovered that the demand for her subject was plummeting and had sensibly decided to become a teacher of English instead.

There was the wife of a French military attaché who was about to be posted to England.

There was a Spanish property agent who found herself increasingly involved in the problems of British expatriates.

There was an incredibly beautiful black Francophone model, originally from Gabon, who had just landed a big contract with a British cosmetics company which was developing new lines for the black market. She was quite happy to keep her French accent for speaking, but wanted to be sure that she understood whatever anyone threw at her in English.

There was an eighteen-year-old Indian girl whose English wasn't up to the standard of the others but who was apparently a brilliant mathematician. An English clergyman who had been sponsoring her through the Save the Children Fund for the previous five years had decided that she deserved an Oxford education. To give her a chance of acceptance by his own college, he was first of all paying my fees for a month's general acclimatisation and study skills, and then proposed to send her to a crammer for the three months before the entrance examination. "She'll sail through on her maths," he'd assured me; my job was to help her settle down to a three-year stay.

The last of the group was a twenty-three-year-old Brazilian. She hadn't bothered to return the questionnaire I'd sent her, which made it difficult for me to work out in advance what she wanted to learn. My first impression had been that her parents were simply so rich that they were scraping around for ways to spend money. So I was almost surprised to discover that she applied herself seriously to the work; but by the end of the first week she had confided that she was in love with the son of a British businessman in Rio. She was chronically unpunctual and had to be reminded three times before handing in any exercise. But I forgave her that for the tactful generosity with which she showered presents on Radhika, the Indian girl, who didn't like to ask her sponsor for spending money on top of the fares and fees he was paying.

The five older women had been quick to grasp my style of teaching and to mesh as a group. That left Radhika, who was young and unsophisticated and completely overwhelmed by the strangeness of the whole adventure. And Mayuko, who clearly understood everything perfectly but found it difficult to let go and speak out. But we still had more than two weeks to go. I was sure that I would break through in the end.

Naturally my pupils have periods of free time when they can wander about Oxford and socialise in an ordinary sort of way on their own if they wish – except, on this particular course, for Mayuko, whose requirement of chaperonage was unusual. But I always lay on a few organised trips as well. A day in London and another in Stratford would come later. On the day of Mort's visit I had arranged an evening out: a drink in a pub followed by a play at the Oxford Playhouse. His warning about the rapist didn't seem sufficient reason to change the plan.

There were eight of us and we could all keep an eye on each other. We were just getting ready to leave that evening – waiting, as usual, for Carmen, the Brazilian – when the telephone rang.

"Whose turn?" I asked; and Mayuko said, "Mine." The rest of us climbed into the Spacewagon outside the front door. After a few minutes Carmen came hurrying out, delighted for once not to be the last.

"Any message?" I said when at last Mayuko joined us.

She shook her head. "For someone who isn't here."

"Wrong number, you mean?"

"Yes. Wrong number. I forgot this phrase."

I smiled. "Never mind. No need to look so worried. Let's go, then."

She squeezed herself in. The Spacewagon is only intended to carry six passengers as well as the driver – which with a group of my normal size is all that's needed. Luckily Mayuko and Radhika were both very thin; and the journey was not a long one.

My male groups always cheer the suggestion of a pub visit, but the women are never so keen. I like to fit it in, all the same, to give them an idea of what to expect if they're ever taken to one. The Vicky Arms seemed an appropriate choice on such a warm evening, so that after they'd looked round inside and had each ordered and paid for a drink for themself, we could all sit out by the river and watch other customers arriving by punt. I'm not really a pub person myself, and don't as a rule expect to recognise anyone in such surroundings; but tonight one face was familiar.

Familiar and ugly. The thug whom I had tipped into Mum's jardiniere was having a jolly time with three of his mates, all of them pretty well tanked up. His private life didn't seem any of my business, but suddenly I stiffened. He had caught sight of Mayuko, who had ordered an

35

orange juice and was trying to sort out the exact change to pay for it.

"That's the one I was telling you about!" Thug's voice was thick, but loud enough to come clearly across the room. "That one over there." He stood up and showed signs of weaving an unsteady path towards her. I moved rather faster.

"Did you tell your friends about me as well?" I asked pleasantly. "But no: I expect you remembered that discretion is part of your job, as well as sobriety."

Sarcasm is wasted on someone who has no vocabulary. He gave a kind of grunting noise and sat down again. Mayuko turned at the sound of my voice, looking strained as she closed her purse and picked up her drink. It's hard for a native to realise what a lot of things there are that a foreigner can't really learn from books. But this was another hurdle successfully jumped.

Carmen, true to form, was insisting on buying Radhika's drink for her. We strolled over to where the others were assembling in the garden. The river, crowded with punters, provided us all with another conversational subject until it was time to drive off to the theatre.

The play was a complicated psychological thriller. To save an extra journey, I dropped Mayuko off at Mum's on the way home. The rest of us had hot chocolate and biscuits round the kitchen table while we discussed whether or not the plot had worked: it was a useful chance for me to see how well they had understood. Maggie hovered in the background, beaming: she loves these kitchen sessions.

After the others had gone up to bed I tapped out a message to remind Maggie that Sasha, Jian-li and Andris would be coming to tea next day, after the court hearing in the shoplifting case. Her smile became even wider. Sasha was one of her favourites, and it was likely that some special baking would go on next morning. As for myself, I was tired. It had been a long day.

I ought to have checked through the telephone tapes; but the answerphone's number display told me that no one had tried to call while we were out, and the wrong number would be interesting only to reveal how Mayuko had coped with it. I went to bed.

The next day started with a formal transaction-type lesson: *I want, would like, I'd like. Can I have? Have you got any?* – together with hints on when it's enough to say *"Return to London, please"* or *"Two to Carfax"*.

Then some practice, with three passengers/shoppers armed with a list of questions along the lines of *Could you tell me where the station is?* and let loose on policewoman, booking office clerk, bus driver and shop assistant. I operated the camcorder so that instead of interrupting them in full flow I could play the video back later and freeze it whenever there was an improvement to be suggested.

Louise, the French attaché's wife, had us all in stitches as the finicky customer who knew just what details she wanted if her new outfit was to be in the latest fashion. That led smoothly into a discussion of British sizing and its foreign equivalents, so it was useful for everyone. We were all in a jolly mood at lunch; except for Mayuko, whose worried expression suggested that she hadn't quite got the hang of the less formal phrases; or perhaps she was shy about seeing herself on the screen.

The afternoon was devoted to a city exercise. Maria, the Spaniard, was given a special assignment: to enquire about renting a furnished property. Each of the others had something to ask for in a shop, and also a travel destination to research. I made it clear that they didn't have to buy anything unless they wanted to, and they certainly weren't supposed actually to make the journey to Edinburgh or wherever. The citizens of Oxford get a bit fed up with foreign students hogging buses and holding up queues in the summer; so each of the group had a different timetable, to stop them all converging on the railway and coach stations at the same moment.

They were going down to the city by bus, so Mum joined us for lunch, ready to do her afternoon duty as chaperone.

"Hold back a bit today, will you?" I suggested to her quietly. "Keep Mayuko in sight, but give her the feeling that she's on her own. Even though you're letting her do all the talking, she may subconsciously be relying on you to get her out of any trouble."

The house seemed uncannily quiet after they'd all gone. No chatter, no barking; not even the clatter of dishes, since Maggie was taking a rest after a morning of baking. I looked forward to the tea party. One reason for despatching the girls into the city had been that the boys and I would enjoy our reunion chat more on our own.

There was time, before tea, for the routine monitoring of yesterday's telephone call. I rewound the tape and switched on.

"Hello. This is The Millstone."

"Hello. Could I speak to Kit? Kit Quilter."

"Who is calling, please?"

"Tilda Grace."

There was a long pause. Then Mayuko spoke in an even more breathlessly tentative way than usual.

"I am sorry. She is at the theatre tonight. Shall I give her a message?"

"Yes, right. Tell her, will you, that I'm back from China. I shall be arriving in Oxford tomorrow for a job interview and a lunch. I'll come to The Millstone at about four o'clock. But I shall only stay one night. Have you got that?"

"Tilda Grace will be arriving in Oxford tomorrow to spend one night only at The Millstone." Mayuko sounded as though she was reading it from a written note.

"Yes. Fine. 'Bye, then."

I frowned to myself in puzzlement and annoyance. It was perfectly in order for Mayuko to have taken a message even although I was in fact still on the premises, but why hadn't she passed it on? She had lied, in fact, when she told me it was a wrong number. Why?

There was no point in making guesses. She could explain when she got back. In the meantime, I wandered over to the coach-house and opened windows. Tilda would make up her own bed when she arrived. All I offered was four walls, floor and roof: room service was not included.

Sasha turned up – alone – much earlier than I'd thought likely. The court hearing must have been a short one: perhaps there had been a plea of guilty. I'd hoped that all three of my ex-pupils would arrive together, for there was a sticky moment to be overcome before I could feel completely at ease with Sasha.

All my students are adults, and although the males are never exposed to the risk of distraction from female students on the premises, there's always me, of course. Naturally I'm extremely careful to avoid entanglements, because apart from the ethics of student-teacher relationships, they would arouse suspicions of favouritism and special treatment. So I can say with hand on heart that on the last night of his course I had not given Sasha the slightest encouragement to open my bedroom door. But the evening, a breaking-up party, had been a boozy one. Sasha was more than a little drunk and so, to be honest, was I. I found him attractive. I was in the mood. All the usual stuff.

What followed was the sort of argument which would

be funny if it wasn't rather sordid instead. I asked him to wear a condom. Not so much for fear of Aids, which he claimed not to have hit Russia yet, but because I had no wish to get pregnant – and I don't stay permanently on the pill just in case the love of my life should turn up without warning.

He said he didn't carry anything of the sort. I offered to supply some. He said – and by this time his need to get cracking was clearly apparent – that he was about to give me the experience of a lifetime and he didn't intend to spoil it for me by letting a bit of rubber come between us. I – about time too – said No.

I had to put up a certain amount of struggle, but it wasn't long before the ignominy of being rejected combined with the effects of vodka and the assault collapsed.

At breakfast next morning we had been at pains not to meet each other's eyes. We hadn't seen each other since then.

I needn't have worried that he was about to spring upon me again after the court hearing was over. Quite the contrary. I stared in astonishment when I opened the door. Here was no sex fiend! If he hadn't been expected, I wouldn't have recognised him.

A few weeks earlier he had been the picture of health and bounce. He'd told me when he first arrived that if he hadn't been picked out for a business career, he might have been a professional footballer. His body was strong and muscular and his face tanned and well fleshed out. He was a good-looking young man with expressive dark brown eyes. Sometimes what they expressed was melancholy, but more usually it was sympathy or a sparkling gaiety. It was in his eyes that his considerable charm was seated. They were not sparkling now.

The young man who first of all shook my hand and

then kissed me on the cheeks three times, Russian style, without passion, had long, greasy, unwashed hair, turning under at the ends like a woman's. His cheeks had fallen in, giving his sad face a gaunt expression, and his eyes pierced fiercely out of two circles of black. I stared at him in horror. Was he trying to make me feel guilty by pretending to be suffering from a broken heart?

"Sasha, are you ill?"

For a moment longer he stared at me as intently as though he were practising hypnosis. Then he threw back his head and roared with laughter. He twisted his hair into a pony tail. He blew out his cheeks and slapped them both vigorously. In his trouser pocket he found an impregnated cleansing tissue and wiped away the dark circles. He was Sasha again, rushing inside to kiss Maggie and dance her round the floor.

"What's going on?" I asked him as we took a stroll round the garden while waiting for the others. I was relieved to find that we had returned to the easy relationship of the pre-seduction scene era.

"I am going to be a great actor. They send to all new students the dates for trials in sports or acting, before our studies begin. The play this year is called Yusopov. With such a title, there must be Rasputin in the cast. I shall take this part. So I am practising. Didn't you say to yourself when you saw me, this man is Rasputin?"

"Absolutely." I was laughing as well.

"In the train from London I saw someone I knew, so I sat down near and stared so." He gripped me by the wrists, turning me to face him, and once again switched on that hypnotic gaze. "No recognition. Not even a wondering, do I know this man? If I don't make my fortune in business, I shall go on the stage. And I shall tell everyone that it was Miss Kit Quilter who gave me my first part. As a young man who wished to open a bank account, I remember.

And then I was the bank manager. I wouldn't give Andris a loan because he had no address."

I nodded; not so much recalling that morning as in approval of Sasha's fluency.

"Well, I'm glad you've gone back to being Sasha for tea. Where *is* Andris, incidentally? I thought you'd all arrive up from the court together?"

"Andris didn't come. He sent a letter to the court, they told me. A medical emergency. I don't think it was true. How can you know an emergency in time to send a letter? He said to me before, he doesn't like to see his name in the newspapers. But it didn't make a difference. The criminals also didn't come."

"You mean they skipped bail?"

"Skipped bail? Is that how you say it?" I could see him feeding the phrase into his memory. "I arrived in Oxford an hour too early, because the next train might be too late. And I went at once to the court, to be sure that the time was not changed. They told me there, the thieves are back in Australia and have sent a cheeky note."

"And Jian-li? Did he turn up?"

"He was on the same train, also early. He walked past me, looking for a seat, but he also saw only Rasputin, not Sasha." He paused to consider. I wondered whether to tell him that he was using the word 'also' too often. But I wasn't his teacher today. "Well, I suppose he saw only the back of my head. So we didn't speak then. He came to the court at the time we were told. We talked for a little while we were waiting, but we didn't stay together. I went to the Ashmolean Museum, to look at pictures, and he said he had more shopping to do."

"You should have come up here earlier," I said. "Instead of hanging about all day."

"Hanging about?"

42

"Killing time. Waiting with nothing to do until the time we'd arranged."

"But I knew you were busy. And I knew also that you have beautiful young ladies with you, who must not see beautiful young men for too long." All my pupils tease me about my insistence on gender separation, although I think they secretly like it.

"But I *have* come early," he added. "Before the time you said. Because I must talk about what happened on the last night of my studies with you."

My cheeks flushed as I remembered that night. "Nothing to talk about. We were both drunk."

"You, perhaps; but I, no. There was a reason why I did not do as you asked. I very much love you and so I want to have a baby with you."

I stared at him, almost unable to believe my ears. The very way in which he said that he loved me made it clear that he didn't.

"I'm afraid that having babies doesn't figure in my life-plan," I said as lightly as I could.

"But please listen while I tell you—"

I shook my head. "Sorry. Nothing personal, Sasha. I'm afraid I'm not interested in any kind of entanglement. With anyone. So we won't talk about that any more, if you don't mind." With no wish for the bedroom scene to be repeated, I turned back towards the house. Now that Griselda was no longer alive to warn of visitors, I needed to be within range of the front door bell – and the sound, when it came, was a relief.

Jian-li was the second arrival, providing a second disappointment. I'd expected all three young men to bounce up to The Millstone, full of their adventures in court and showing some pleasure at seeing me again. Sasha's brooding act had made him almost unrecognisable when he first arrived, although by now he was his usual self once more. Now Jian-li too seemed to have changed since our last meeting. The shape of his face, with its high, chubby cheeks, always gave to Western eyes the impression that he was smiling, but I could see from the edgy movements of his eyes and hands how annoyed he was by the cancellation of the court hearing. Even before he greeted me he was pouring out the story which I already knew.

"This journey is not needed. Why do they not tell me before I buy ticket?" His English was still as stilted as ever, in spite of all my efforts: perhaps part of the strain which showed in his eyes could be explained by the problems of living in a foreign country. "I am not happy to come again to Oxford, so far. I have much to do." His agricultural college, I knew, had arranged for him to have two months' work experience in Kielder Forest before term began, although the time might have been better devoted to recognising that English has more than one tense.

"They paid our expenses," Sasha reminded him.

"You look as though you've spent yours on new clothes, Jian-li. Very smart." I was trying to smile his annoyance away – and it was true that he looked as though he had stepped straight out of a fitting room. His jeans were so new and stiff that they seemed to be holding up his body without help from his legs.

Remembering his manners, he moved his mouth and cheeks into a smile, although his eyes still flickered with indignation. "Yes. There are sales, with Reduced Bargains. I am shopping because too early for tea."

"Talking of tea, come and say hello to Maggie. She's got a marvellous feast waiting for us."

Like all my pupils, he thought Maggie was wonderful. Perhaps it was because she didn't ever expect any of them to talk to her in perfect English. He chose to drink jasmine tea, which was a bit naughty. People who give other people Fujian Oolong ought to do their bit towards getting rid of it. But I didn't hold it against him for more than three seconds, and the next couple of hours passed happily. Sasha ate enormously, and I did my share. Jian-li had never pretended to think much of Western cooking, but Maggie had made some little almond cakes which she knew he liked, and he emptied the plate almost without noticing.

Only a few minutes after they left, the first of my girls started to return, proudly brandishing their notes on fares and pick-up points and where they would have needed to change had they really made the journeys. They always returned from these expeditions in a state of excitement; and today for the first time even Radhika, the young mathematician, was eloquent with pleasure.

"I was three times asked by American tourists which were names of colleges," she said. "And every time I answered correctly." I had taken the whole group on a tour of most of the colleges in their first week, before making Radhika undergo an interview by each of the other six as they pretended to be admissions tutors. There was so much pleasurable chatter that it was not until almost supper time that I realised Mayuko had not returned.

Perhaps Mum had driven her straight back to Heyford Close from the coach station, which should have been her last point of call. It wasn't very likely, because breakfast was the only meal due to be provided there. But it was possible that Mayuko had felt ill and asked to go straight back and to bed.

But in that case surely Mum would have phoned to explain. I tried ringing her number, only to be greeted with an infuriating warble. A few years ago I gave her a dual-purpose fax/telephone for Christmas so that she could communicate with Maggie. I ought to have been more generous and installed a new line and a separate fax, because all too often she forgets to switch back to the telephone mode after sending a message.

I gave it a few moments in the hope that she'd hear the warbling and realise what she done. But a second try produced the same result and although I then put a written message through, asking her to call me at once, there didn't seem much chance that she'd see it immediately.

Perhaps she was having a cosy G & T with Mrs Mallory, her next-door neighbour; I rang the number on the off-chance. No luck. At that point – rather belatedly – it occurred to me that Mum had come up to The Millstone by car but had travelled into Oxford with Mayuko by bus. I checked it out. The car was still parked in the drive.

Now I was really worried. Ought I to start phoning round hospitals? Yet even if there'd been some kind of accident, surely two people wouldn't be completely laid out at the same time. It was necessary to do a little thinking. That earlier mention of the risk of kidnap, which I had thought so far-fetched at the time, invaded my mind. And was the thug really on Mayuko's side? Even if he was genuinely working under Uncle Shin's instructions, there were such things as wicked uncles.

Ought I to phone Mr Tanaka to find out whether he knew anything about it? He would report straight back to Tokyo and there would be a huge flap. I was in a certain amount of flap myself, but there must be some simple explanation.

Someone would have to be left in charge while I tried to find out what had happened. Maggie would cope with supper, because she always did, but it might be more important than usual that any telephone messages should be accurately passed on. Had Tilda arrived yet, I wondered, and hurried to the coach-house to find out. It was empty and tidy, exactly as I had left it. Damn.

Of my six pupils, I chose the Finnish teacher, to take charge. Louise was more fluent, but tended to get excited. Stolid Marjaleena could be trusted to take a conversation slowly, write everything down, make sure that any caller left a telephone number and generally act as house mother while I was away. I explained that I was worried about Mayuko and that I would keep phoning back to see if there was any news.

It was a lovely sunny evening at the end of a lovely sunny day. I ought to have been offering myself a refreshing Pimm's in the garden. Why yes, Kit: what a very good idea! Instead, I sat for a moment in the car, puzzling, before I started the engine up. Andris hadn't appeared, Tilda hadn't appeared, Mayuko hadn't appeared, Mum hadn't appeared. What on earth was going on?

Chapter Four

The Heyford Close cul-de-sac was jammed with cars trying to turn in impossible places as parents picked up their whiter-than-white children from the tennis club. I remembered now, one of the reasons why Mum had been able to help out with Mayuko was that there was always a gap in her coaching while the annual junior tournament was in progress. I barged my way bad-temperedly through, yelling out of the window about consideration for residents, and grateful that I was driving the little Renault instead of the Spacewagon which I use for group expeditions.

The house was empty. Mum and I keep each other's keys, in case of emergency, so I was able to let myself in, but it was clear that she hadn't been home since lunch: my faxed message was still dangling. The calendar hanging in the kitchen showed nothing unexpected for the day: '*Oxfam 10 – 1. Mayuko 2 – 6. Lunch?*' I went upstairs.

Lying on the table by Mayuko's bed was a diary, and I had no compunction about opening it – but she had written it all in Japanese, naughty girl. The only entries of possible interest were a couple of telephone numbers: a London one and another which I recognised as French. I copied them down. It would be easy to find out by ringing them who was on the other end of the line, but it wasn't the right time to do that yet. Confessing that Mayuko was lost was the kind of humiliation I could do without.

Mayuko's travel exercise had been to find ways of getting to Bristol. Tomorrow she would be expected to play the part of a travel agent and tell one of the other students which route was quickest, which was cheapest, which was most convenient if she was carrying heavy luggage, all that sort of thing.

Following the timetable laid down for her, I went first to the railway station. The chap at the information desk remembered her all right. He'd tried to explain that she would have to change at either Reading or Didcot, and had given her the two relevant timetable leaflets to take away. But she didn't seem able to cope with them, so that in the end he had written down the details of the next possible train – but had noticed that she didn't move on to buy a ticket. As far as he recalled, she was alone, so Mum must have been obeying the instructions which I now regretted.

A couple of shops should have come next, but of course they were closed by now, so I moved on to Gloucester Green to investigate the coach station. The ticket sellers had changed since the afternoon, but I struck gold in the shape of the girl at the forward reservation desk, who had come on duty just before four o'clock. "Yes, I saw a Japanese woman. I noticed her because she was on her own, and almost always they come in pairs or groups. She was asking all these questions and writing the answers down in a notebook. The queue behind her was getting longer, and Mike was looking really fed up. I heard him yell out, 'Look, make up your mind. If you're going, there's a coach just about to leave.'"

"What happened next?" I knew, of course, that Mayuko wasn't going anywhere.

"She turned round with a funny expression on her face. I wondered whether she was angry, thinking Mike was being rude, but he wasn't really, only trying to help.

49

Maybe it was just that she couldn't make up her mind. It's difficult to tell with foreigners, isn't it?"

"So she went out of the building?"

"Oh no. She turned back to Mike, just as the chap waiting behind thought he was going to get a bit of attention at last. I suppose she bought a ticket, though I couldn't really see. And then she ran for the coach."

"She did what!"

"I should think she only just made it. I heard the despatcher send it off only a few seconds later."

Christ Almighty! What did Mayuko think she was doing? Where did she think she was going? And why? I would have to check every stop along the route. I thanked the girl nicely and established what time all this had happened.

"Did you see anyone else get on the coach after her?" I asked.

"I can't really see from here who boards which coach. There was a man at the next window who bought a ticket but then looked uncertain about whether he was going to travel or not. When the girl dashed for the door he seemed to make up his mind and he went in the same direction. I don't think they were together, though. What's all this about?"

I mumbled some story about a passenger who hadn't arrived in Bristol, and thanked the girl for her help. Just as I was leaving, she called me back.

"I've remembered something else as well. There was a woman. She'd been sort of browsing around my desk for quite a bit – picking up timetables more as if she wanted to find out where it was possible to go, if you see what I mean; not actually interested in the times. She was quite old, really, but she suddenly took off like she was doing an Olympic sprint. She didn't have a ticket, but of course the coach driver could have

50

sold her one. She didn't come back, so I suppose she got on."

Good for Mum; though she wouldn't think much of that 'quite old, really'. Well, that was some kind of relief. There was a lot of explaining to be done; but Mayuko hadn't been kidnapped and sooner or later I ought to get a message and with any luck no one else need ever find out about the escapade. I fished for a phonecard and rang The Millstone.

Marjaleena answered beautifully. There had been a call from my mother. She and Mayuko were staying at a hotel in Bristol, whose telephone number she had given; she would ring me again at ten o'clock. I was not to worry.

I worried; but what worried me more as I trudged back to the car was whether Maggie would have kept some supper for me. Of course she had: chilled vichyssoise soup, coronation chicken and summer pudding. And there was a bottle of white wine in the cooler, which we shared in friendly silence.

The call came punctually at ten.

"Kitten. Did you get my message? I'm terribly sorry about this. If I'd been a bit closer, listening, of course I'd have stopped her . . . It took me by surprise, I'm afraid."

"I'd specially asked you not to stay close," I reminded her. "What's Mayuko's explanation for all this?"

"She said she thought she was supposed to make the journey after she'd chosen which method was the best."

"That's not true. They all understood perfectly well . . ."

"Yes, I know. And the next pretence was that she longed to travel through the English countryside and the temptation was too much for her."

"A likely story!"

"So then of course – we were on the move by this time

– I said that we could get off at Cheltenham and take the next coach back and then she'd have had her trip. That was when she produced story number three, which was that she had a special desire to visit Bristol."

"Poppycock! I shouldn't think she'd ever heard of the place before I dished it out as her test destination. I had to show her where it was on the map. What do you think is *really* behind all this, Mum?"

"She's worried about something. Frightened, even. I mean, until now she's been very polite and amenable; but today, even when I gave her a direct order to get off the coach, she wouldn't. I didn't feel I could physically manhandle her, so in the end there didn't seem anything to do but go along. I got a very definite impression, Kitten, that she wanted to get out of Oxford for a little while, and stay out: but she wouldn't say why. I did wonder whether it might have anything to do with the thug. She caught sight of him last night, apparently."

"Yes, I know. I was with her. But there was nothing to link—"

"I mean, she caught sight of him skulking outside the house. He hasn't come back inside the garden again since you taught him a lesson, but he does still hang around."

I considered this for a moment. It was true that to see the same bruiser face twice within a few hours might be worrying for her, but the reaction was all wrong. She should have discussed it with me. Taking off into the blue wasn't going to solve any problem. But Mum was still talking.

"I've explained to her how inconsiderate it was to go off without a word and not even send a message when she arrived here. She's very contrite; genuinely, I think. I couldn't persuade her to come on the phone, but she'll apologise when she gets back."

"Which will be when?"

"In time for lunch tomorrow."

"OK. We'll sort it out then. Thanks a lot, Mum. Make sure she pays all the bills."

For a little while I puzzled over the affair without coming to any conclusion. Then I went to look in the telephone record book. I don't have a payphone for the students, although that would probably be a sensible thing to do. Instead, whenever they make a call they're expected to write down the date and time, the number dialled and the number of units used. At the end of the course I get an itemised statement from British Telecom and use it to bill them.

To my surprise – since I'd asked her not to use Mum's phone – I found that Mayuko had made no calls at all to Japan, although I would have expected her at least to report to her uncle that she was safely ensconced. But she had rung each of the numbers which I had copied from her diary. The second call – to the London number – was made while we were all waiting to leave for the Playhouse and she should have been hurrying to join us. I frowned over that second call. Acting on impulse, I rang it myself.

The hotel receptionist who answered waited to learn which extension I wanted.

"I had a message asking me to call your number," I fibbed. "But they forgot to say who was calling."

"We have two hundred and fifty guests here tonight," the receptionist told me helpfully, in case I'd considered asking her to go through the list. I thought quickly, and realised there was only one person whom I knew for sure was in England and acquainted with Mayuko.

"Do you have a Mr Fergie staying?" I asked.

There was a short pause before she said brightly, "I'm putting you through."

I put down the receiver quickly before she could make

contact. Although it sounded as if a happy ending were on the way, there was no point in letting anyone know that I had temporarily lost my precious charge.

Ten minutes later, Rufus rang me. Telepathy at work? Or, finding himself connected to a dead line, had he asked himself who might have been calling.

"Hi, Kit! Everything all right?"

"Fine, thanks."

"Great. Kit, I've just been trying to speak to Mayuko, but I can't get anything except a kind of bird song noise on the number you gave me."

I laughed and explained about the switching system on Mum's fax machine. "They'll realise what's happened as soon as one of them wants to make a call out. Would you like to leave a message with me?"

"No need, thanks. I only wanted to have a chat; make sure everything's going smoothly. She'll be at your place as usual tomorrow, I take it."

"There's an out-and-about exercise in the morning." I was getting pretty good at producing quick lies. "From about two in the afternoon she'll be here. But if it's only for a chat, I'd rather you waited till the evening instead of disturbing the class."

"Yes, of course. 'Bye, then."

I had preparations to make for the next morning's lesson, but the evening had proved tiring, so instead I set my alarm for half-past five. That was how I came to be not only awake but dressed when the front door bell rang at six.

The visitor was Mort, but he was not alone.

"This is Detective Chief Inspector Drew," said Mort formally, and I found myself having an ID card thrust under my nose, just as you see on the telly. "Sorry to disturb you at this hour. I told him you were an early riser. As I have reason to know."

He was pretending to make a joke, but neither of the two men was smiling. My stomach began to churn. Something must have happened to Mayuko!

"Do you want to come in?" I asked faintly. Stupid question: of course they did. There are only two chairs in my office so I led the way into the drawing room and pulled back the curtains.

"I'd like to ask a few questions about a Miss Grace," said the detective. "Is she a pupil of yours?"

I blinked in non-comprehension. Why were we talking about Tilda? I had been so certain that the problem, whatever it was, must concern Mayuko that it took me a few seconds to move on to a different track.

"No. No, she isn't."

"But you know her?"

What on earth could she have done? Tilda was not an altogether admirable character. She was selfish and flirtatious and less considerate than she ought to have been in making it clear that any flirtation could be considered at an end, but those were hardly criminal offences. Smuggling, perhaps. Had she brought something back from China against somebody's laws? It's a bad habit of mine, speculating about possibilities when all I have to do is ask for the facts.

"Yes, I've known her for a long time. What's happened?"

"When did you last see her?" It seemed that the facts were only going to emerge in the detective's own good time.

"About two years ago. She's been working in China."

"You mean she doesn't live here?"

"She has a kind of pied-à-terre." I explained about the coach-house. Only now for the first time did it occur to me that with so much else on my mind I hadn't made a second visit on the previous evening to see whether she'd turned up or not.

"That would explain this." The detective pulled a plastic bag from his pocket. Inside was enough of a torn luggage label to reveal that Tilda's destination had been The Millstone. My head swam dizzily as I stared at it. Watching television had introduced me to the uses of plastic bags, as well.

"Please tell me," I said faintly. "What's happened to Tilda?"

"I'm sorry to have to tell you, Miss Quilter, that your friend is dead."

It wasn't possible. I stared at him, refusing to believe it.

"The bloody rapist." Mort thought he was muttering under his breath, but it brought down on his head as impressive a snub as a detective inspector could deliver.

"That's making an assumption for which as yet we have no evidence."

"Are you telling me she was raped before . . . before . . ."

"We don't know yet. Her body was found in a cutting off the Oxford Canal. It's being examined at the moment, and until the examination is complete we don't even know whether drowning was the cause of death. I'm sorry to have brought you such upsetting news, Miss Quilter. If you're prepared to allow PC Goodison into your kitchen, a cup of tea might be helpful."

I nodded. Mort knew the way.

"As you can imagine, it's important for us to trace her last movements before she died, and you're the best person to help us. You were expecting her here?"

I nodded again. "Not till the afternoon. She'd got a lunch date, with a job interview before it. I expect she was hoping to get a few weeks' work at one of the Oxford language schools before going abroad again."

"What time did she plan to arrive in Oxford?"

"I didn't speak to her myself. One of my students took the call. I've probably still got it on tape, if you'd like to hear it."

"You record your telephone calls?"

"There are special circumstances." I didn't feel like going into details. Mort could fill him in on Maggie's disability and my teaching methods. "You'd better come into the office."

It didn't take long to find it. Luckily there had not been enough telephone traffic to finish the tape and record over the call. Only thirty-six hours had passed since Tilda, alive and cheerful, had been making plans for her future. As I'd expected, the detective asked to take the tape away.

"So who beside yourself would have known that Miss Grace was due to arrive in Oxford yesterday?"

It was hard to give proper attention to questions like this. The shock of what I had been told was getting worse, not better, as it began to sink in that I should never see Tilda again. I had to force myself to think.

"Presumably the person who was going to interview her. And the friend she was meeting for lunch. But if you mean who at The Millstone, only the student who took the call. And she – a Japanese girl called Mayuko – only arrived in England ten days before, so it wouldn't have meant anything to her."

"When this student eventually repeated the message to you, was anyone else within earshot?"

I paused, trying to look as though I was making an effort of recall. What I did remember was that Mayuko had said it was a wrong number and had deliberately not passed the message on at all. That was the moment when for the first time I began to wonder whether Mort had been right in his assumption that the rapist was responsible.

"No," I said. "Nobody." Well, in a sense that was a truthful answer.

We moved into the kitchen, where Mort was ready to play mother. There were a lot more questions. Most of them revolved round my lack of anxiety about Tilda's non-arrival in the coach-house. I stopped feeling upset and sick and started to be angry at the suggestion that I ought to have worried more. By the time he asked to interview Mayuko I was sufficiently in control to say that she was away on a visit and that anyway since he'd heard the tape there was nothing to add. Perhaps making me irritated was a form of psychotherapy; but I didn't really believe that Detective Inspector Drew was as subtle as that.

If he had been trying to help me come to terms with the news he brought, he didn't succeed. I took them across to the coach-house and helped them to find the address of Tilda's father. But after they'd left, the shock really hit me and I found myself shaking like an over-ambitious jelly. Tilda and I had been best friends for the three most important years of our lives, sharing plans and hopes with a closeness which could not be affected by anything which had happened since. She was only twenty-nine; a reasonably conscientious teacher, but someone who believed in having a good time outside working hours. A woman who didn't take anything too seriously, but liked to tease. Bubbly: that was the word for her. Always looking forward to the future. And now there wasn't any future any more. When Maggie came down to start on breakfast, she found me being sick in the kitchen sink.

That morning the students didn't get their money's worth. The police had stolen my lesson preparation time. But I've been teaching for so long that naturally I have plenty of session schemes on file, so we slogged away at conditionals and I doled out worksheets. I didn't have the energy to make it fun.

Mort came back just before lunch.

"Thought you'd like to know, Kit my love, seeing as how she was a friend of yours. She wasn't raped."

"Yes. Thank you, Mort. That does help a bit. I don't know why it should, when she's dead anyway."

"Death by drowning is what they say, after a blow on the head. But I still reckon it's the same chap. Someone had her round the throat before she fell. There are bruises to show. He must have jumped her, like he did the last one, and held on too tight when she put up a fight. Just bad luck it was her. Could have been anyone."

"Where did it happen?"

He fished a battered city map out of his pocket and pointed. "Up at the end of Fisher Row, off Hythe Bridge Street. See that footpath? Runs between trees; goes over a little bridge. Underneath the bridge there's a sluice control. Lets the water off if it gets too high in the canal. It was open after that storm we had. Seems her body was thrown in on the canal side, and the force of water pushed it partly through. It was wedged under the bridge; difficult to see."

"But why would she have been there, Mort? Where does the path lead?"

"Bit of wasteland waiting for development, with a car-park one end. No, she'd be there by mistake, most likely. Never enough taxis at that time of day. She'd be walking to the Cornmarket to get a bus. Missed her way."

That didn't make sense. It was two years since Tilda had last clocked in at the coach-house, but she wasn't likely to have forgotten the way. That path was on the wrong side of the canal and there was no bridge across which would have gone anywhere near the buses except Hythe Bridge Street itself.

"What time of day was she killed?" I asked.

"Between nine and ten, they reckon. That would fit with her getting in from Paddington on the 9.12."

After two years in China, she would have luggage. She would have waited for a taxi, even if it took half an hour. But then I remembered that she had an interview and lunch lined up. It might have been convenient to leave any heavy stuff at the station and call back for it later. I told Mort that it would be worth checking the left luggage. But I still didn't go for the rapist theory.

"You told me before that all the earlier rape victims were Asian," I reminded him.

"That's one of the things makes me reckon it's the same fellow that we need to look for. Granted, your friend looks English enough from the front. But she was small. Slim. With that sort of neat, short hair that they wear over there, judging by what you see on the box. And the big thing is, she was carrying a grip – cabin bag size. We found it in the bushes. The one with the torn label. And the bag was covered in, what do you call them, characters? Chinese writing, anyway. Bought it out there, I suppose. Seeing her from the back, anyone might think she was Chinese."

"But this chap you're after, has he ever attacked in daylight before?"

"Not that we know, no. But you know how it is. Every time they get a girl, it goes to their head and they want another one quick."

"No, I don't know how it is." And I didn't believe it either. It seemed clear as daylight to me that someone had either persuaded or forced Tilda to take that secluded and little-used path and had then deliberately killed her. I couldn't imagine who and I couldn't imagine why. But what seemed equally clear was that the police were never going to find him. Or her, since genderism is out of fashion. One of these days, no doubt, they would catch their rapist and then, because their minds were already closed, would close the file on Tilda's murder too.

Why should that have made me uneasy? Because I don't like loose ends? No, there was more to it than that. When someone who has been part of your life suddenly isn't there any more there needs to be a reason. There needs to be someone to blame and someone to punish. If the police weren't going to find that someone on their own, then I would have to see what I could do to help.

Chapter Five

Skipping lunch was no hardship: I didn't feel like food. Returning to the coach-house, I found an address book of Tilda's and worked my way through it. She must have spent the night with someone in London after flying in from Beijing. And someone else in Oxford must have wondered why she didn't turn up for lunch after her interview.

But all the crossings-out in the book made it clear that I was following a dead trail. TEFL teachers are gypsies on a world scale – if even gypsies were allowed to be called gypsies any more. Travellers, then. All Tilda's English friends were travellers. A year or two here, a year or two there – and July and August are the usual changeover months. Any of these names, whatever the addresses or telephone numbers which Tilda had written beside them, could have been in London or in Oxford this week. Especially in Oxford, where language schools practically take over the city in summer.

I tried another tack, listing Tilda's movements over the past nine years in the hope that some memory would click into a useful place. The major jobs were easy to remember. A year in Spain. A year in Cambridge – that was when she was still hoping to get Rufus out of Libya. Then two years each in Mexico and Turkey. The next year had been a messy one for her. Rufus, free again, had taken her out to Japan at the end of August and by the time they split up she was too late to get work for a full academic year and had to make do with a few months in Italy. After that, the two years in China.

My pen hesitated over that brief stay in Japan. Might she have met Mayuko there? Yes, just possibly she might, but where would that get me? Mayuko would only have been fifteen at the time – and, in any case, had been under my eye in The Millstone at the time Tilda was murdered. Had she needed an alibi, I was it: but it was absurd to think that she did.

Right, then; what about the summer jobs? TEFL teachers abroad are badly paid and tend to blow what savings they have on making exotic journeys in the countries they are just about to leave. They have to work their way through what ought to be a summer vacation and, luckily for them, this is when foreign students pile into England. It wasn't so easy filling in this part of Tilda's timetable, and there were several gaps in my list; but one place brought to me a halt for a second time.

Bournemouth. Tilda, I knew, had been teaching in Bournemouth when Rufus arrived back in England. I was sure of that because at his request she had chucked in the job before her contract ended. She had had enough of a conscience to try to find a replacement for herself, and I was one of those she approached. I couldn't do it for her, but I remembered the date. I had come across Bournemouth in some other connection recently. It took a little thought, but in the end I remembered where.

Sasha had taken an intermediate English course in Bournemouth, and it must have been just about three years ago. And Sasha had said, hadn't he, that there was someone he knew on the train to Oxford. Someone who hadn't recognised him with his Rasputin face on. Might that someone have been Tilda? But even if it were, why . . . ?

Fact before fantasy. A real detective would no doubt have taken off for Bournemouth, but I had only half an hour left before taking charge of the afternoon teaching session. Tilda had listed all the addresses to which she'd ever applied for work on a separate page, so it didn't take long to find the number I wanted. Back in my office, I picked up the phone and started asking questions.

From the reaction at the other end of the line, three years ago might have been in the Dark Ages. Even with the help of a computer it took some time for staff listings to be married to pupil listings. But I did eventually establish that, yes, Sasha had been in Tilda's class for six weeks. There must have been a black-listing code against Tilda's name, because the secretary was able to remember that the school's principal had been very fed up at losing one of her staff without notice and, with a little nudging from me, eventually came up with the information that Sasha had been upset at the change of teacher and had pestered her to find out where Tilda had gone.

Where did that leave me? A little thought persuaded me that I would have to behave like a detective after all. To put blunt questions to Sasha over the phone was not likely to reveal any truths. I knew that until his university course started he was spending a few weeks in the offices of the company which was sponsoring his business studies. So I rang him there with some cheerful guff: it had been so nice to see him and I had to be in London that evening and could I take him out to dinner? There was nothing strained about his voice as he accepted.

What did I expect to discover? And if he did have any guilty secrets, did I really want to know? I liked Sasha very much indeed. There was something about his particular variety of charm that made me want to protect him. The mere fact that he had once known Tilda wasn't any reason for killing her, and it was hard to imagine such an open-hearted young man creeping up, pouncing, squeezing . . .

Or was it? For most of the short time I had known him he had been cheerful and almost unnaturally optimistic, considering that his homeland was collapsing before his eyes. But there had been one Saturday night when he came home drunk from a pub, grim with despair at the thought that he would one day have to return to St Petersburg. I'd always understood that Russians were perpetually homesick away from their motherland, but Sasha's enthusiasm for everything British was enough to persuade even a Brit that we weren't quite on the rocks yet.

Another memory. Some kind of quarrel with Jian-li one evening after dinner. They had been talking politics: the successes and failures of communism, I think. It became personal. Jian-li was scornful of Sasha's longing to stay in England, to rat on Russia. For his own part, he intended to return to help his country's sytem work. That was how he put it, anyway. I knew – from Tilda – enough about the strength of nepotism in Beijing to suspect that, as the son of a political high-up, he might be hoping to become something important in whichever government ministry dealt with forestry.

Anyway, the argument between the two of them took place. This was outside teaching hours and I wasn't listening properly; but when Sasha thought his honour was under attack, he'd gone for Jian-li as though he were in a wrestling ring. They were both strong and fit and determined to win, but it was Sasha who came off second-best.

The next day I'd caught him setting up some kind of booby trap for Jian-li, and had to be pretty sharp in making it clear that this was meant to be a friendly course. He'd abandoned what he was doing at once, laughing in his usual easy way and kissing me on both cheeks as he assured me that it was only a joke. Now, considering Tilda's death, I thought quite hard about that booby-trap. And I wondered exactly how Sasha had spent his day in Oxford before turning up at The Millstone for tea.

There would be no need to leave for London until six, and my pupils deserved more of my attention than they had received in the morning. We moved into the billiards room and started to act out the travel agency scene for which they had prepared on the previous day. To make it more complicated, I gave each of them a few sentences which had somehow to be worked appropriately into the conversations, to use all the conditional forms they'd practised in the morning.

They didn't know anything about Tilda, of course, and they were an exuberant group. Although I couldn't join in the laughter, I forced myself to give the session my full attention. That – and the fact that there were six of them in the room, the size of my usual class – is probably why at least an hour had passed before it occurred to me that Mayuko had not in fact returned as Mum had promised.

The tape recorder was running – and anyway, by this stage in the course they were all becoming confident enough to correct each other and discuss the correction as a group. So I excused myself for a few moments to make a phone call. In the quiet of the office I first of all tried Mum's home, without success, and then rang the Bristol number which she had given me the previous evening. From the hotel I learned that Lady Quilter and her young companion had left after breakfast. They had ordered a taxi to take them to the station, but in fact had used a minicab which happened to arrive while they were waiting. There was a tinge of criticism in the voice which provided this information: as well as giving a taxi driver a wasted trip, Mum had no doubt deprived someone of a tip for opening a door. That was not how a Lady was expected to behave.

I frowned slightly over the minicab, which could have had no legal right to pick up someone who hadn't ordered it; but its convenient arrival must have suited both parties. Mum had said on the phone that they'd take a train back, so my next call was to BR to discover whether there had been any hold-up on the line that morning. This time the voice on the other end of the line was quietly boastful: the two most likely trains had been respectively one minute late and two minutes early. So what could have happened?

Back in the billiards room, I found everyone in fits of laughter. Radhika had successfully negotiated her visit to Edinburgh and now Louise, departing from the script, was demanding a trip to the moon. Marjaleena, whose straight face disguised a strong sense of humour, showed no surprise as she slowly but successfully worked in some of the grammatical constructions I had set.

"If you travel via Mars, it will take a little longer but you could make a stopover on Venus if you wished."

"I see. If I missed the take-off, would I have my money repaid?"

"Try, 'get my money back'," I suggested automatically. "More colloquial." As a rule I'm careful not to interrupt these role play sessions while they're in progress. Any corrections can come later, when I play the tape through and try to elicit improvements from the students themselves. But today my mind was only half on the conversation, causing professional standards to slip.

"Would I get my money back?" Louise repeated, and then broke off as the telephone began to ring. "My turn, I think."

I stayed close, ready to take over the conversation if

it proved to be Mum. Louise, after asking as usual for a message, frowned as she tried to understand it.

"You are worried about a cat?" she checked. Her glance at me was an appeal for help. I took over.

"Hello. This is Kit Quilter speaking."

The caller was Mrs Mallory, who reminded me – as if I hadn't known for years – that she was my mother's next-door neighbour.

"I'm always most particular about not feeding Pippa unless I'm specifically asked to take responsibility for a weekend," she said in that clipped North Oxford voice. "Encouraging cats to desert their own homes is a most unneighbourly action, in my opinion. But the poor animal is clearly starving. She's been in and out of her cat flap a dozen times today, and now she's sitting in my garden mewing in a manner which I find most distressing. I can get no response from your mother's house, so I propose to offer Pippa a saucer of milk and a little steamed fish."

I bit back the response I would have liked to make. Anyone with an ounce of neighbourly feeling would have begun by worrying about the cat's owner rather than the cat itself. However, since I knew that Mum was not in fact lying at the bottom of the stairs, unable to move, I thanked Mrs Mallory kindly for her offer and promised that any investment she was good enough to make in tins of cat food would be repaid.

Louise, meanwhile, had been passing on to the others that part of the conversation which she had heard.

"This is the second call about cats today," commented Radhika.

"What do you mean?" I demanded. "When was there another one?"

"While we were eating our meal. You were not with us."

I was startled and annoyed. I ought to have checked

whether anyone had phoned when I was in the coach-house – but then, Radhika ought to have told me. I said so.

Upset by my obvious irritation, she hurried to explain.

"It was not a sensible call. A joke, I am thinking. There was nothing to tell you. Someone who pretended to be a cat. Miaow, miaow. I'm sorry if—"

I was already dashing for the door.

"It's OK," I said. "You couldn't have known. Just carry on, all of you."

Back in the office, I rewound the tape and played it. As Radhika had claimed, it began with a soft mewing which certainly could not have meant anything to her but was a clear message to me. When I was a little girl, this was the way that telephone conversations between Mother Cat and Kitten had always begun. This was Mum trying to get in touch with me. And it must mean that she was in trouble: not supposed to use a telephone; having to hope that if any sound was heard it would indeed be ascribed to a cat.

The whole recording lasted only a few seconds. The mewing began as soon as the receiver was lifted. It was interrupted as Radhika gave The Millstone's number and asked who was calling. The line went dead almost as soon as she finished the question.

I played that part of the tape over and over again. Mum knew my system. She could be sure that sooner or later I would listen to any message she managed to pass, and so it seemed certain that there would be a message there. There must have been a reason why she didn't dare wait until Radhika finished speaking.

It wasn't easy to isolate whispered syllables from beneath Radhika's much louder voice, but I was soon pretty certain that the second of the first two words was "caravan". With the first one I could only be confident

69

of an "ee" sound. Free? Tree? In the end, almost sure, I settled for "green". Once Radhika stopped talking and waited for a response, the message, although still desperately faint, was easier to hear. "Fourteen minutes from hotel." Then the line went dead.

My heart thumped with anxiety. Fear of kidnappers had never entered my thoughts before Mayuko's arrival, but then, probably I had never had such a seriously rich pupil before. It was Rufus who had got me worried even before she arrived, with his insistence that I should not tell the others her surname, that she should never be photographed, that there should be no publicity of any kind about her presence in Oxford. It was for the same reason, he'd said, that the visit was fixed up with such speed. I'd gone along with all this, playing my part as promised, but never really believing that anything like this could happen. I would never have involved Mum had I thought there was any danger.

Who else, apart from me, had known who and where Mayuko was? The prowling thug who had been hired as a bodyguard must have guessed that she was someone special, but he did seem to have thought only that he was protecting her from the local rapist. The Japanese ambassador apparently knew who she was, and Tanaka and perhaps others of his staff had known where she was. At least, they did while she was in Oxford, but she would hardly have given them warning of her flit to Bristol. That left Rufus; but since Rufus had been involved in arranging the visit, he would want it to be successful.

All the same, I couldn't help hesitating over Rufus. It was a long time since we had last met as friends, and longer still since we were lovers. For old times' sake I would never have done anything to let him down, but I couldn't be quite sure that he would feel the same about me. I shook that thought out of my head and dialled the hotel number which I had found in Mayuko's diary. If he was indeed involved in her disappearance in any way, he would know about it already; if he was not, he ought to be told.

The snooty receptionist regretted that Mr Fergie was no longer a guest at the hotel. There was nothing necessarily sinister about that: he had told me that he would be travelling around. It was just that anxiety was making me suspicious about everything at this moment.

What about the police, then? I knew that they didn't regard it as their business to worry about adults who were temporarily missing unless there was some compelling reason to believe that harm had come to them. Would they accept two hardly audible phrases and a few seconds of cat-imitation as such a reason? It didn't seem likely. If this *was* a kidnap, then sooner or later a ransom note would arrive. Only then would there be evidence that a crime had been committed.

There was something else niggling at my mind. Why had Mayuko taken off from Oxford in the first place? As the police would undoubtedly point out if I tried to involve them, there seemed no doubt that she had gone of her own accord. Something had alarmed her: that seemed clear enough. But if she feared strangers, she would have been safer with me. Why didn't she realise that?

All these thoughts took only a few seconds to pass through my mind; and even as I worked out priorities I was listing what I must do. It was crazy, I suppose, to travel to Bristol in the hope of tracking down a minicab and a green caravan, but I couldn't bear to sit and do nothing.

My first call was to a friend, Janet, who like me is a trained TEFL teacher. She was eight and three-quarter months pregnant and bored stiff with sitting at home waiting. Yes, she'd be delighted to take over my group for a day. She joshed me a bit about cracking up and then fell silent as I started loading on one or two extras, in the form of important telephone calls to be received. If my mother phoned, Janet was to get an address quickly, without wasting time on chat. If Rufus Fergie phoned, he must be told that it was essential for him to leave a number where he could be reached.

"What's up, Kit?" she asked.

"I can't tell you. I don't really know myself. There may have been an accident of some kind. I just need to be sure that any calls which come in are dealt with sensibly. I'll phone in as often as I can."

Returning to the group, I told them that Mayuko had misinterpreted yesterday's instructions and had finished up in Bristol; I was worried about her and proposed to fetch her back by car. I gave Janet a good puff to make it clear that the course wouldn't suffer, and announced that the telephone-answering rota would be suspended while she was in the house. While waiting for her to arrive I put Maggie in the picture as far as it concerned her, which wasn't very far. Then I made a series of phone calls which eventually, after a good deal of holding the line, please, produced the addresses of licensed caravan sites around Bristol. For good measure, I was given a list of mobile home parks as well.

Janet arrived, walking with a careful waddle as though the baby might fall out if she were too energetic. I showed her my course scheme, performed the necessary introductions and promised that Maggie would put clean sheets on my bed for her. Then I was off.

The journey took less than two hours, and my first stop after arriving in Bristol was the hotel. Nobody had noticed anything special about the minicab except that it was red; it had looked just like an ordinary car. The receptionist provided me with a list of minicab firms and I spent half an hour on the payphone. Although the cab hadn't been ordered by the hotel, its arrival there must surely mean that it had been some passenger's destination. But apparently that information only went on the record when a call went out to find the nearest car to a new fare – and it was already clear that this particular driver hadn't been too fussy about picking up passengers on the spur of the moment. So there was no joy there.

Next question was about phone calls. Lady Quilter had made two calls from her room; those would both have been to me. More interesting was the fact that her young Japanese companion had come back into the hotel after going out to the taxi and had tried to use the payphone in the lobby.

"She couldn't cope with it," the receptionist told me. "I could see she was having trouble, so I actually put her money in and dialled the number for her."

"I suppose you don't remember . . . ?"

"It was a London number. I can't say more than that."

I fished for my notebook and offered her the number of the hotel in which Rufus had been staying.

"Yes, that was it!" she exclaimed, pleased that she could recognise it.

Why? I asked myself after I'd thanked her. Why should Mayuko be so meticulous about keeping in touch with Rufus when she was so casual about reassuring me? I'd had Japanese pupils before and they'd always shown an excessive politeness to teacher. There was something very odd about Mayuko's behaviour. I even began to wonder whether she hadn't been kidnapped at all, but had herself helped to lock Mum up for a little while in order to prevent something or other being discovered. If that were the case, then probably I had nothing to worry about – but it didn't make much sense. Certainly that hypothetical scenario wasn't plausible enough to make me give up the search and merely wait for the wanderers' return.

As I was turning to go, the doors of the hotel restaurant opened and the head waiter appeared, menu tucked under his arm, to indicate to the starving masses that he was open for business. I was a starving mass myself after skipping lunch, but I had too much to do before darkness fell to take time off now and walked resolutely back to the car. Only then did I remember that I had a dinner date for the evening. In London.

I looked at my watch. Sasha would long ago have left his office and I had chosen a rendezvous which was convenient for car parking, not for telephone contact. I must remember to apologise next day; he would be prickly about being stood up. Well, who wouldn't be? It was hard to remember that only a few hours ago the most important question in the world had seemed to be: who murdered Tilda? Now the most urgent question was nearer home. Where was Mum?

Chapter Six

It had been intelligent of Mum to time her journey, but the fourteen-minute guide was not of much immediate practical use. Bristol's traffic routing system surely qualifies it for inclusion in a book of labyrinths. I had a book of city street maps in the car, but within a few minutes of leaving the hotel I was grinding my teeth in frustration. It might have helped, of course, if I had known for sure where I wanted to go.

Unsurprisingly, there were no caravan sites in the middle of the city. The three nearest were across the river from Clifton, so I decided to start there and then take what looked like some kind of ring road to the south-east, where there were two more.

The quickest way out of the chaos was across the Clifton Suspension Bridge. I raided my meter-money store to pay the fifteen pence toll, and left two more coins handy for the return trip. Now I could start the fourteen-minute countdown. Almost at once, as I drove on, I found myself in a peaceful area of woods and playing fields. It was a relief not to have impatient drivers pushing at my bumper as I struggled to navigate, but even the sight of open spaces did little to relieve my increasing depression. This was a wild goose chase: it would only be a matter of time before I had to admit it.

Leigh Downs, the first site on my list, was a cheerful family park. The August evening was still warm, and outside nearly every occupied caravan the debris of open-air suppers was being cleared away. I found only one which was locked up and silent; and even as I considered it, a car drove up and disgorged two adults, three children and five helpings of fish and chips. The only question I found it necessary to ask at that site was where the family had found the fish and chips.

The answer – assuming that the mobile van stayed where it was, opposite the George at Abbots Leigh – was on the way back towards the city, so I tightened my belt for another hour while I set out to polish off the other two sites on my list. One was a haphazard, amateur sort of place – no doubt belonging to a farmer who'd chosen this means of diversifying. No neatly-outlined plots here, with electricity hook-ups and taps. Just a sloping field in which you could park where you liked. The seven caravans in occupation offered magnificent views across the river, but I wouldn't have wanted to tow one of them uphill to the gate on a rainy, muddy day.

The farmer's wife appeared almost before I'd switched off to tell me that there was water available outside the house and milk, eggs, cheese and other produce on sale at the farm shop, and the barn could be used for shelter in wet weather and children were welcome to come and stroke the livestock. She was so desperately eager for custom that I felt mean as I merely asked whether she had seen a Japanese girl in her field within the past twenty-four hours. She hadn't: each of the caravans was occupied by a family staying for a week.

Site number three was run like a military camp. A barrier across the entrance brought me to a halt while the gatekeeper came out to check my resident's pass. Lacking any such credential, it was necessary to produce another story. I had come to collect my mother, who had been spending the day here with a friend. Unfortunately

76

I didn't know the name of the friend or the number to the plot, but if I could just drive through I was sure that my mother would be looking out for me.

This wasn't good enough to get the Renault past the barrier, but I was allowed to march up the main thoroughfare under escort. Half-way along I made the mistake of mentioning that, according to my mother, the caravan was green. We came to a halt.

"Then you've obviously come to the wrong site. There are no green caravans here. I'll take you back."

"No, hang on a moment. Maybe what she meant was that it was called Green-something."

"Touring caravans don't usually have names. Probably what you want is Leigh Downs. Turn right out of here and—"

I didn't bother to listen. Leigh Downs was where I had started. But I wasn't too upset at being hustled out. No one, surely, would try to get someone unwilling, like Mum, into a set-up of this kind.

There was something else to disturb me. The gate-keeper was right to point out the lack of names: I had noticed it for myself. Equally noticeable was the fact that I hadn't seen a single green caravan on any of the three sites. Coffee and cream were the fashionable colours this year. Well, perhaps every year: this was not my area of expertise.

By now I was really hungry. I'm a black-coffee-only woman at breakfast time, so it was well over twenty-four hours since I'd last eaten. The fish and chippery wasn't on my direct way home, but I made the necessary diversion. Then, after pointing the car in the direction of the bridge again, I pulled into a space in front of some lodge gates. The meal wasn't exactly up to Maggie's standards, but as I licked each finger in turn I felt a little of my energy returning.

I'd intended to make use of the facilities at my last stop, but the gatekeeper's attitude had discouraged that idea. The overgrown bushes of a neglected drive provided an adequate alternative. It was getting dark by now, but even so it seemed only proper to move out of view of the road. I went through the open gates and found a private spot.

I was still smoothing down my culottes as I stepped out on to the drive again, but that didn't prevent me from seeing something unexpected on the other side of the drive. A notice board, too shabby and faded to read from a distance in the dusk; so that it was only curiosity – and perhaps a reluctance to take to the road again – which moved me across to read it at close quarters. There were enough letters still decipherable for me to be sure that what it proclaimed was Greenleigh Residential Park.

Greenleigh! Green! It wasn't on the list I'd been given of mobile home sites, which was what this must have been. But the dilapidated notice and the run-down state of the approach road suggested that the site was no longer in use – and so a far more sensible choice than a field swarming with happy campers if you were trying to hide someone. Would Mum have been able to read a notice like that if she was being hustled past it? Perhaps, if someone had had to pause in order to open the gates. Anyway, worth exploring.

I set off on foot. If the drive proved to be very long I could come back and take the car nearer, but for the moment a silent approach seemed wise.

The ground sloped gently downhill – not towards the gorge, but into a valley which ran at right angles to it. I turned a corner and came to a halt. On either side of the road, about a hundred yards ahead, twenty or more unbeautiful structures which were surely too large ever to be mobile were perched on concrete blocks. The drive continued to curve, so there might even have been more round the corner.

The nearest of the mobile homes was dilapidated to the point of danger, its roof even more sieve-like than The Millstone's. It had once had a little garden, but now the hedge was tall and lanky and there were nettles growing in the flower bed. My eyes took in the details, but my real attention was pitched a little way ahead. Although most of the other homes had an equally abandoned look, there was a light burning in the window of one of them.

It could have been just a squatter. A New Age traveller tired of traipsing round with the rest of the gang. A tramp happy to have even a leaking roof over his head. All this I told myself sternly; but I couldn't prevent my hopes from rising.

Stepping off the concrete drive, I approached quietly through the long grass. Luckily I always wear trainers for driving: no one could have heard me coming. Pressing one's nose against a window has always seemed to me a stupid way of snooping, although it's good for a scream in films. I came to a halt a little way away and at an angle. That gave me a good enough view, but I reckoned that I would be invisible unless someone turned off the light and actually came to stare out of the window.

The source of illumination was one of those powerful torches which motorists are recommended to have handy for changing wheels at night; with a firm base but adjustable direction. What it illuminated now was the back and side view of a man sitting in a canvas garden chair and talking into a portable telephone. As I watched, he came to the end of his conversation, stowed the phone away in a leather pouch slung on a strap across his shoulder, looked at his watch, pulled a balaclava helmet over his face and picked up the lamp.

I could follow where he went next by the movement

of the light. It was clear that a mobile home, unlike a caravan, was divided into rooms, and none of the windows was curtained with anything more than cobwebs. When he came back again, he pulled off the balaclava, and that was the first time I had a clear glimpse of his face. It was the thug: the prowler I had caught in Mum's garden.

His next move was a good one from my point of view: he fitted a Walkman headphone to his ears. Now I could take the risk of making a sound. Moving cautiously in the direction taken by the light a few minutes earlier, I came to a halt beneath another window and began to mew.

Two mews to start with, and then a wait for the response. To my delight, it came at once. "Miaow, miaow."

"Mum." I pressed my lips close to a crack where the window frame had warped away from the wall. "Can you hear me?"

No answer. Perhaps she was afraid of alerting the thug to my presence.

"It's all right," I hissed. "He's got earphones on."

"He's just going out to get fish and chips."

"Right. I'll wait."

The wait was not a long one, although every second dragged. Within ten minutes I heard the sound of an approaching car. It came not from the road but from the opposite direction, round the curve: a red Ford with a crumpled front bumper. As it paused, the thug hurried across the grass, got in and was driven away.

The front door was fastened not just by a mortice lock but with a padlock clasping two metal bars. My hopes that the wood would prove rotten were unfounded – all I got when I hurled myself against it was a bruised shoulder. Back to the window, then, which had warped sufficiently to give me leverage. I forced the whole frame out and squeezed myself gymnastically but inelegantly through. It was a tight fit even though I'm pretty slim and under-endowed in the bust department. I couldn't see Mum getting out that way. She's got a good figure for a fifty-year-old, but all the same . . . Never mind, there would be a larger window somewhere which could be opened from inside.

"Thank God I've found you. We haven't got long." The fish and chippery, as I well knew, was only a few moments' drive away. I felt my way over to give Mum a hug and realised at once that she wasn't hugging me back.

"Handcuffs," she said succinctly. "Fastened round some kind of pipe."

I'd brought the torch from the car in my pocket and took it out to examine the position. Mum was sitting on the floor of a shower cubicle, necessarily straight-backed with her arms strained tightly and painfully behind her.

"The bastard!" I swore, testing the handcuffs. They were high-class security issue and I could tell at once that I had no hope of forcing them open.

"He only fixed me like this while he went out." She sounded almost as though she was excusing him, though I suppose her motive was to reassure me. "What does he want, Kitten? Who is he?"

"Didn't you recognise him?" Now I was hauling at the pipe to which she was fastened. When so many of the structures on the estate were rotting away, it seemed hard that this one should hold together so well; but presumably the kidnappers had looked for the one in the best condition.

"No. He always puts that hood thing on before he talks to me."

No doubt that was just as well. Mum would be safer if the kidnappers thought themselves unrecognised. I explained that her gaoler was the prowler from her garden.

"Mum, they'll be back soon and I don't think I can get you out without proper tools. I'd do better to leave you here, with no sign that anyone's found you, while I get the police. Will you be OK for another half hour?"

"Make it twenty-five minutes," she said, managing a smile. "But anyway, clever Kitten to find me."

"Clever Mother Cat to get at the telephone." We rubbed cheeks, and for a second time I did a dive head first through the opening. Once outside, I pushed the window back into place. It hadn't fitted snugly to start with, so I hoped that no one would notice any extra draught.

I kept off the concrete driveway, in case the car returned, and made as much use as possible of the shelter provided by trees and other mobile homes as I hurried towards the road. As it came into sight, I stopped dead. What an idiot I was to leave the Renault so conspicuously near the gate. Why on earth hadn't I gone back to move it after discovering the notice board? Well, it was too late to regret that now. The kidnappers could hardly have failed to notice the car, but perhaps they had assumed it to contain a courting couple.

For a moment or two I kept very still, so that if anyone was prowling round I would hear him. Then, with the key ready in my hand, I made a dash for the driver's door.

As I broke cover and stepped out on to the concrete a pair of headlights were switched on, dazzling my eyes. The Ford must have parked on the other side of the road, waiting for my return. Now the driver revved the engine with a vigour suggesting that he was driving a stolen car and came straight for me.

All those pupil-lessons in karate and judo and fair and foul wrestling paid off, even though fighting off cars had never been on the syllabus. Instead of panicking I rose on to my toes and checked my balance. At the last minute but one I side-stepped to the left. Only when the headlights had committed themselves to that change of direction and were almost upon me did I make my dash to the right.

No time for click-clunking a seatbelt. I flung myself into the driving seat and shot off with as little regard for the gearbox as if I too were joy-riding. The engine gave a cough of protest and took for ever to pick up speed, but at last I was moving.

And thinking. I remembered from studying the map that there was a village just off this road. But the nearest house – and telephone – might be some way away, and the road would be dark and deserted. It seemed safer to head straight back to the suspension bridge. It was not too much further on, and there would be traffic on it; people to act as witnesses and so to discourage anything that wouldn't bear witnessing. I didn't want to be caught; but on the other hand I did need to be chased, because otherwise my pursuers would return to Mum and move her before I had time to organise a rescue.

Why wouldn't the Renault go faster? Because it was cheap and old and underpowered, that was why, and it was probably only my anxiety which made me feel I must pump the accelerator harder than usual. The Ford had had to turn round, which gave me a necessary few seconds' start, but I saw it coming up fast behind me just as the great pillars of the bridge came into sight.

Approaching the toll gate, I realised that I had just passed a telephone box on the right-hand side of the road. Had it been an old-fashioned scarlet one, I might have seen it in time to stop; but its glass sides were almost invisible until the last minute. It would be safer to press on. No doubt there would be another box at the far end of the bridge. Besides, I had my toll money ready. With any luck, my pursuers would be held up at the barrier while they searched for change.

No such luck! They charged straight at it, snapping the

bar. For a second time the Renault gave its discreet little cough, and now I was definitely slowing down. Coasting, in fact. I swore with frustration – and only then did I realise what had happened. Expensive cars have little red lights to flash when incompetent drivers are about to run out of petrol, but my cheap job had let me drop in the mess of my own making. Usually I fill up before any motorway journey, but today's programme had been unscheduled. As I came to a halt, the Ford crashed into me from behind. Harder than it meant to, no doubt, since the driver would have assumed me still to be moving. I ought to have fastened that seat belt after all: there would be a bruise on my forehead to point the lesson.

The bump had jerked the Renault forward. Now the Ford was coming up for a second go. I hurled myself out on to the road, staggered for a moment and began to run, ready to flag down the first car that came towards me.

Nothing appeared. Where was everybody? Turning my head, I saw that I was being followed by the thug. To judge by the noise, the Ford's driver was trying to untangle the bumpers, but when I next looked round he had given up and joined in the chase, leaving the two cars to block the carriageway.

What a wide river the Avon was! I can jog for ever, but I was running too fast – and too soon after eating a generous helping of chips: I could feel a stitch preparing to immobilise me. Why was nobody driving out of Bristol? It was only ten o'clock and somebody, surely, must live on the far side of the gorge.

There *was* someone on the bridge. Not far ahead I caught a glimpse of two young men dressed entirely in black. They were not in a car. Not even walking. In fact, the word that came to my mind was 'lurking'; and even as I caught sight of them they seemed to disappear into the shadows. But never mind, they were human beings who could have no possible connection with my pursuers. "Help!" I panted as I stumbled on. "Help!"

Shouting was a mistake, for by now the footsteps behind were closing on me and I ought to have used what breath I had left to run faster. The thug hurled himself at me from behind in a rugby tackle and brought me crashing to the ground. Hard, concrete ground which bruised and winded me – and to make it worse, he stamped on my wrist with a force which made me gasp with pain. To lie still would leave me open to more damage. I used the side of the bridge to pull myself up and, staggering slightly, turned to face him.

"You!" he said, and that one word told me how much trouble I was in. I was someone who could identify him. I could easily discover his name from Mr Tanaka if left free to do so. On top of that, he had a score to pay off for his humiliation at Heyford Close.

For a moment we faced each other, circling like professional fighters, neither wanting to make the first move. What had happened to those two young men? I had thrown the thug once and was confident that I could do so again – but his friend was coming up fast and two against one would certainly be too much for me. Taking a deep breath, I screamed.

It wasn't a scream of fear. When I'm really frightened my throat dries up and not even a squeak emerges. This was an actor's scream, demanding attention.

It worked. The circling movement meant that the second kidnapper was behind my back, which was dangerous, but the two young men were in view, which was good. They emerged from their hiding place and one of them began to run towards me. The other seemed at first to be reluctant to move, but responded, even if unwillingly, to his friend's shout of "Come on, Tom!"

They weren't going to arrive in time, for the bout

had started and I could tell at once that this was one I wasn't going to win. The effect of the tackle and the earlier bump on my head was to dull my co-ordination. I didn't feel strong. I didn't feel confident. All I could do was play for time. I managed to twist myself out of his first two holds, and hooked his ankle hard enough with my foot to bring him down on one knee. Then, with fingers stiffly extended, I lunged towards his eyes in the manner advocated by women's self-defence classes.

It wasn't something I'd ever been able to practise on anything but a dummy, and the effect was terrifying. Roaring like an animal, he grabbed hold of my wrists and swung me first of all sideways and then into the air. I braced myself – or rather, relaxed my muscles – for the moment when he would crash me down on to the ground. But he didn't do that. Instead, as he flung me upwards and outwards, he let go of my wrists.

I was not going to land on a nice soft judo mat. I was not even going to land on a bone-cracking road surface. I was going to land at the bottom of the Avon gorge.

Chapter Seven

When I felt myself sailing into the air, it wasn't so much panic which overwhelmed me as disbelief. This couldn't be happening to me. Not to *me*.

Fortunately, it didn't take long for the disbelief to be banished by an instinct of self-preservation. As though I were a gymnast doing incredible things in the air after a vault, I twisted and turned my body, willing it to corkscrew back to safety. My eyes were dazzled by the lights which picked out the shape of the suspension bridge and made it seem to float high above the river like a spaceship. The sharp metal points which were intended to discourage potential suicides banged against one hand and slipped away before I could hook it over them.

A wide strip of metal curved out from the top of the balustrade before turning under the pavement of the bridge. Still twisting, I flung out my other hand, gripped an edge of the support at the place where it became horizontal and, with a jerk which must have dislocated a shoulder, checked my descent. But I was on the wrong side of the bridge: the outside.

Fear is a great painkiller. If my shoulder and wrist and hand hurt, I wasn't aware of them as I began desperately to swing my body from side to side until there was a chance of grabbing for a second handhold. Just as I made it, a figure appeared above me. It was one of the two young men: the one who wasn't called Tom. He was dressed from ankle to wrist in close-fitting black – the dry equivalent of a wet-suit – with an elaborate body harness strapped over it to make him look as though he'd stepped out of a science fiction film. "Hang on," he called.

I was hanging on, all right, and he was stretching down to grab my wrists. But before he could get hold of them he was knocked sideways, out of sight. By the thug, I suppose. I could hear the sounds of shouting and fighting; and also, at a distance, of a car – at last – screeching to a halt. None of it seemed to have anything to do with me. My own world was a silent one. I couldn't call out, couldn't scream, could hardly even breathe. Every cell of my body was concentrated on the need to hold tight. The Clifton Suspension Bridge is 245 feet above the river.

From somewhere above me came a shout. "Tom! Check my clip!" Almost at the same moment, the young man in black suddenly appeared beside me on the outside of the bridge. Instead of dangling, like me, he was in an abseil position: feet pressed against the side, legs pushing out, body bent in a V, one hand grasping the edge of the balustrade, the other hand reaching down towards me.

It was too late. My brain was still sending frantic orders to my muscles to hold tight, but they had suffered too much damage and the signals weren't getting through.

"I'm going," I said. And then I did scream, because as I began to slither down the side of the bridge, my would-be rescuer let go of it and hurled himself towards me. It was crazy. It was suicide.

"I've got you," he said – and so he had, for his arms were linked firmly round my waist. But all that meant was that we were falling together. Down, down, down – faster and faster.

"Hold on to me if you can." His mouth was near my ear. I couldn't grip with my hands, but I moved my arms under his shoulders.

"That's fine. You're going to be all right. I'm in harness."

I didn't know what he meant, but I'd given up caring. Had I been falling by myself I would have panicked, screamed, flailed at the air. But his grip was tight enough to be ridiculously comforting. We were about to die together, but in an odd way it didn't matter. Rather, it was exciting. The ultimate adventure. I shut my eyes, buried my face in his chest, and waited for the crash.

"We're going to get wet." That statement sounded as absurd as his assurance that I was all right. "It's the extra weight, you see. Hold tight."

We hit the water as he spoke. When an Olympic diver pierces the surface from a great height, he seems to enter as smoothly as a pointed knife penetrating butter. Our descent was more like a hammer hitting steel. I'd never realised that water could be so hard. Every bone in my body seemed to judder as we went under. But I was still held in that embrace which had promised me safety.

The movement changed its nature. Now we were being tugged out of the water like a recalcitrant cork: emerging reluctantly at first but then with a sudden pop which sent us flying up into the air again.

The young man in black laughed aloud. "Isn't it fun!" he said. "Always the best moment, when you realise that the elastic band hasn't snapped. My name's Bodger, by the way."

I opened my eyes, hardly able to believe that I was still alive. We were shooting upwards almost as fast as we had descended.

"Marvellous, isn't it?" he exclaimed breathlessly.

Now we were at the top of the rise and began to fall again. Yes, he was right: it was marvellous. While we were in the water, Bodger – what sort of a name was that? – had managed to tuck one knee between my legs to make me feel even more secure than before and his grip round my waist was tighter than the most passionate of embraces. To make up for my useless hands I crooked my elbows more firmly under his arms. This had become a sexual experience, made more intense by the aphrodisiacs of fear and relief. At once excited and at peace, I surrendered my body to the exhilaration of the rise and fall.

At last the bouncing ended. Still suspended on the end of the line we came to rest, merely swaying and turning in the breeze. In the stillness I became aware that I was panting aloud as though an instant love affair had been ecstatically consummated – and even through the strong body harness I could tell that Bodger had been affected as strongly as myself.

"This is a new game," he whispered. "We must try it again together some time." Then his voice took on a more businesslike note. "The next bit may be tricky. Usually there's a system for getting back on terra firma, but I didn't have time for the usual drill. In other words, no safety rope or rescue boat. How's your head for heights? Can you bear to look down? I've still got you."

It was nothing to do with heights which made me reluctant to move. My face was nuzzled into Bodger's neck and I would have liked it to stay there. However, it was as well to remember that I was still dangling in the air with a nasty drop below. I looked down.

The Avon itself was a ribbon of black; but there was a road running beneath the bridge, along the side of the river. The headlights of cars driving along it illuminated patches of the bank. It looked a long way away.

"Now then," said Bodger. "If we were absolutely confident that the goodies were winning up on the bridge, we could wait while someone lets down a rope and hauls us up, or else sends for the SAS. But we're not. It wouldn't be impossible for one of your villains to unhitch me, and then we'd both be in trouble. Would you be prepared to take a tumble? I can swing you down and sideways. It'll take two or three goes, but I reckon I could get within nine or ten feet. Of course, I can't guarantee a soft landing."

"You're the boss." I wouldn't like to say that I was happy about the prospect, but I trusted Bodger to do the best he could for me.

"Off we go then." It became clear within the first second that he was an expert at dancing in the air. I had my eyes open now and could see the diagonal line for which he was heading.

"Time for you to let go," he said on the third descent. "I'm just about to move my leg." Now only his arms were holding me. "Next time down I shall push you off. Relax. Relax. Your body's made of jelly. Go!"

It was a short fall; hardly more than six feet. The tide was out, so I landed on a bed of mud. There was a moment of panic as my face sank into what felt like a quicksand and I was unable to breathe. But with a squelch I managed to extricate myself and clear first my mouth and then my nostrils. My shoulder was painful and – more worryingly – there was still no feeling in my hands; but as far as I could tell, nothing more was broken.

A swishing sound made me look up. In the darkness I saw Bodger's descent only at the last moment, as he unclipped himself and dropped neatly down beside me. The lights of a car briefly picked us out as he helped me to my feet.

"I was going to kiss you," he said lightly. "But I think perhaps I'll wait until you're a bit cleaner."

"I don't understand how you came to be there," I said faintly. There was a lot more I didn't understand – such as how I could still be alive – but the biggest miracle was that of his perfectly-timed appearance on the outside of the bridge.

"All questions will be answered in due course; but first things first. You're to stay exactly where you are while I get hold of an ambulance. It may take a minute or two, but don't move."

"And the police," I said urgently. "I need to talk to the police."

His voice indicated reluctance. "I should think somebody up on the bridge will have reported an attempted murder by now."

"It's not that." It was the thought of Mum, handcuffed and helpless, waiting to be rescued, wondering what had happened to me. "I'll explain later. But it's terribly important. The police first."

"OK." He helped me through the clinging mud to a piece of driftwood on which I could sit while I waited.

"You'll come back, won't you, Bodger?"

"I'm not likely to abandon you now. But I may not actually come back here, to this spot; not if you're wanting a heart-to-heart with the police. To be honest, they and I are not best friends. They seem to think that people who play dangerous games cause them a lot of trouble, whereas really all we want is to be left alone to look after ourselves."

"You saved my life. They couldn't possibly—"

"Yes, they could. I'm a fully-paid-up member of the Dangerous Sports Club and therefore a known criminal; under warning already. You can talk as much as you like about this gallant young man you've just met, but don't mention my name, there's a love. I shall be hanging around in the shadows to make sure that someone does turn up to look after you. And then I'll come and see you in hospital. Promise." Already he was moving away.

"How can you visit me in hospital when you don't even know my name?" I shouted after him.

"How indeed!" He laughed, walked squelching back to me and kissed me in spite of the mud. "Right: let's be formal."

"My name's Kit Quilter and I live in a house called The Millstone at Headington, in Oxford."

"I can see that you're still afraid that I'm going to run out on you. Nothing could be further from my mind. Quite apart from wanting to build on our special relationship, I'm longing to hear what exactly led up to you being tossed into the gorge. See you!"

The darkness seemed darker after he had gone, and the silence more silent. On the road above there was both light and noise, and as time passed it was tempting to struggle up towards it. But I did as I'd been told and stayed where I was until at last I heard the sound of a police siren. The car stopped a few yards short. As the beams of torches began to search the bank I stood groggily up to show myself. I'd been wearing a white blouse at the beginning of the afternoon, but now it was black with mud. "Here!" I shouted.

Two policemen arrived above me, contemplating without enthusiasm what was about to happen to their shoes.

"I can walk," I called out. Optimistically, as it turned out. The mud clung to my feet and, losing my balance, I fell forward into a crawling position. The policemen hauled me out.

"There's an ambulance coming," said one of them, in case I had any ideas of transferring my filth to the back seat of their car. "Just give us your name, and we'll follow you up to the hospital and take a statement there."

"There's something important first. Will you get through to your station and tell them? My mother's been kidnapped. I can tell you exactly where she is. It's

93

a disused mobile home park on the other side of the river. Called Greenleigh Residential Park. She's being held in the third one down on the right. She's handcuffed and she may be in danger. Get someone there at once, please."

The two policemen looked at each other as though I were mad.

"You need to take it easy for a bit, miss. You've had a bad fall, by the looks of it. Lucky to be alive, I should say. Suppose you start by telling us your name and address and then we'll get the rest of the details later."

"My mother's name is Lady Quilter and she's in danger!" I shouted. "You've got a radio or a telephone, I presume. Before you do anything about me, please get this going. It's urgent."

Still they wouldn't move. They'd probably arrived expecting to be greeted with relief and gratitude, and were taken aback by my truculence. "Your name, to start with," one of them repeated.

"If you don't get this through to whoever's in charge of your detective branch I shall raise such a stink that you won't know what's hit you. Even if you can't bring yourself to believe me, for God's sake pass the buck to someone who's senior enough to give an order. Now!"

I can hardly have looked a very commanding figure, wet and filthy as I was and hunched over to relieve the pain from my shoulder. But the sheer intensity of my demand must have helped to persuade them that they had nothing to lose by passing the message on. One of them returned to the car and began to speak into a microphone.

"Young lady here; accident victim or PS," he said, when he had identified himself and established contact with whoever he was calling. "Worried about her mother, a Lady Quilter." He looked towards me. "Would you like to repeat the details, miss?"

94

I would have liked to snatch the microphone from his hands to speak into it directly, but my fingers still wouldn't obey me. Instead I gave him the facts by dictation, one sentence at a time.

"Lady Quilter has been kidnapped. She is handcuffed to a pipe in a mobile home. In Greenleigh Residential Park, which is disused. On the west side of the Avon, within a mile of the suspension bridge. She's in the third mobile home on the right, going downhill from the road." I didn't know the area well enough to give the name of the road. "And the two men who snatched her are probably on their way back now to move her somewhere else. They must have ten minutes start, so please get a move on."

There were other things I wanted to say, but I held back until I reckoned that the chap at the other end had had time to get things moving. It was tempting to mention that a second kidnap victim might be somewhere on the abandoned estate; but to ask an already dubious police force to search for a Japanese heiress who had never been reported missing might cause them to write me off as a complete nut. When they found Mum as a prisoner they would have to believe that dirty work was going on – and Mum could tell them about Mayuko. I chose a minor detail to add:

"The car used by the kidnappers is a red Ford with a crumpled front bumper," I told the two officers then, sending one of them back to his radio. "Probably other damage as well, since it smashed through the toll barrier. And if you're imagining that I jumped off the bridge, you're wrong. I was thrown off." I didn't know what they'd meant by saying I was a PS, but it seemed more likely to stand for possible suicide than postscript. "Hasn't anyone reported that there was a fight up there?"

Silently I answered my own question. Probably not. Judging by Bodger's reaction, Tom would not have chosen to involve the police, and the motorist whose car I had heard might have arrived too late to see what was going on.

"My car is up on the bridge," I added, and gave them the licence number. "They smashed into it." I reckoned then that it would be only kind to divulge the information which the policemen would need to make their report. "My name's Kit Quilter. Address: The Millstone, Headington, Oxford."

A second siren, at first distant but soon so closely shrill that it seemed guaranteed to frighten anyone who was faintly off colour into a heart attack, announced the arrival of an ambulance. As it screeched to a halt the back doors were flung open and an ambulanceman jumped down and began to pull out a stretcher.

"I can walk," I said for a second time – and for a second time I was wrong. "Your body is made of jelly," Bodger had told me, as a warning that I must not be tense when I fell; and now his instruction had taken effect. The bones of my legs had melted and the muscles had slackened. The whole of my body was trembling: yes, just like a jelly.

"You're going to be all right now." A comforting voice was repeating another of Bodger's reassurances – although a few moments passed before anything actually happened. Behind my back, questions were being asked of the police. Had I lost blood? Had I been moved since the accident, whatever the accident was? Had I moved myself? Yes, I had. No obvious signs of neck or spinal damage.

"Shoulder and hands," I said out of the depths of an overwhelming weariness. My head had sunk to my knees and I was incapable of raising it. Two pairs of hands, gentle but firm, took hold of me and raised me on to the stretcher. I was lifted into the ambulance and left to lie for a few seconds, staring up at the roof, while more information was exchanged outside. Then doors closed, and we were off.

It seemed important to keep awake, but even a dim light was too strong for me. My eyes closed.

Chapter Eight

Little by little I came back to life; and rather wished I hadn't. As I was wheeled into a hospital on a trolley, my forehead was aching, my shoulder was aching, my neck and spine and ribs were aching. Even my hands were no longer painlessly numb. That was a good thing, I supposed; but it left me feeling that what I wanted now more than anything else was a knock-out dose of painkiller from which I could awaken in a few days' time feeling as good as new.

Naturally I didn't get my wish. My face was swabbed clean, and for a short while there was a fuss of attention: my pulse was taken, joints were hit with tiny hammers, limbs were cautiously moved, various parts of my body were prodded and a bright torch was shone into my eyes. But it didn't take long for someone to decide that I would be able to survive a bit of normal neglect. The tedious business of X-rays and more questions and the necessary clean-up proceeded at a leisurely pace. It felt as though several hours must have passed before my various wounds were all finally bandaged, strapped or plastered. At every possible opportunity I enquired about my mother; but the hospital and the police force were not in communication.

A woman police constable came at last and told me that Lady Quilter had been found and was at this moment drinking cups of strong tea at the police station. Since

I'd already decided to leave Mayuko's abduction to be reported by Mum, that was all I needed to know. I then allowed myself to sink into the peaceful cocoon of painkillers and sleeping tablets. The WPC did her best to keep me awake for long enough to extract a coherent statement, so I described how I had found my mother handcuffed and accused her abductors of ramming my car and attempting to murder me. When it came to reasons for the abduction I murmured that my mother could say more about that, and by the time I was asked how I had escaped death my eyes were closed and I was doing a heavy breathing act. Whether or not she was fooled, she let it go; and within a few seconds it was no longer an act.

I awoke next morning to find Mum sitting beside my bed.

"Kitten, darling! Is there any bit of you I'm allowed to hug?"

"I don't think so." I needed a moment to carry out a mental exploration of my own body. My left shoulder and arm were tightly bound, and the four fingertips of that left hand – the thug's stamping ground – emerged pinkly from a plaster cast. My right hand merely had a kind of compress bandaged on to it. At some point in the middle of the night I had been told that it was not broken but merely bruised and strained. "Oh Mum, I'm so glad you're all right. I was worried they might not get there in time, the police."

"Gary and Clint and Rambo didn't bother any more with me," she told me.

"Who are Gary and Clint and Rambo?"

"That's what they called each other, the three who locked me up in that place. Thought they were being very clever, I'm sure. The one we caught in the garden was really Mike: the code slipped from time to time. Anyway, they didn't come back after you'd left."

"And Mayuko? Do you know what they did with her?"

"Not for certain, I'm afraid. But judging by the short time it took for Mike to be picked up after he'd made his phone call, I'd guess she was being held pretty near. I know you didn't want any publicity about her, Kitten. But I felt I had to mention her to the police at once, while there was a chance of finding her."

"Yes, that was right."

"You may need to push them on that. They did promise to search the whole estate, but I'm not sure that they believed she really existed."

"I should have thought the fact that you were handcuffed . . ."

"People play kinky games these days." Mum is as conventional as middle-aged women come, but her comment emerged in a matter-of-fact way. "Anyway, I told them that I didn't know her surname: all I did know was that she was rich. They'll be wanting a lot more information from you, no doubt. And as soon as you find her, I think you'd better send her home. Acting as her chaperone has been slightly more exciting than I bargained for."

"Yes. I should never have asked you. I'm terribly sorry, Mum. I never thought . . ."

"Don't worry about it now." She bent to give me a gentle kiss. "Tell me what's been happening, Kitten. I don't mean about Mayuko, but how you got into this state. No one in the hospital seems to know. Was it a car crash?"

"No. Although your Hollywood friends did do their best to ram me off the road. I'll tell you all the gory details later, and you must tell me how they got hold of the two of you. But would you do one thing for me

100

first? Call The Millstone." I explained about Janet, who was holding the fort for me. "Take any messages that have been left. I specially need to know if there's been a call from Rufus Fergie, so that I can get in touch with him."

While she was gone I had time to survey the row of plastered legs on either side and exchange smiles with my nearest neighbour. Then a pair of nurses arrived, drawing the curtains round before they helped me on to a commode, washed my face, made the bed and informed me that I'd slept through breakfast, but that they'd see what they could do.

"And your brother's here to see you," one of them said as she was leaving. "It's not really visiting time yet, but since he's come such a long way and your mother's here already, Sister said he could be allowed ten minutes."

"Thank you," I murmured. I haven't got a brother. Mum was about to get a shock when she returned to find an unknown son waiting to greet her. I was already grinning when Bodger came into the room.

This was my first opportunity to take a good look at the young man who had saved my life. He was no taller than myself, with a solid, muscular body. His sandy hair had recently been smoothed back with a wet brush, but was already beginning to spring back into its natural curliness again. Above wide, strong cheekbones, his eyes were a light blue – and focused on me with interest and approval.

Like Mum, he was careful not to hug me as he kissed every part of my face except for the bruise on my forehead.

"Not only brave but beautiful!" he exclaimed.

"You're not allowed to make me laugh. It hurts my ribs. Bodger, I can't thank you enough for what you did last night. It was incredibly—"

"It was seriously nothing," he said, sitting down beside

101

me. "I knew it was safe, you see. Usually there's an introductory lesson, of course. Not everyone gets thrown in at the deep end like you. You may have thought I was plunging to destruction beside you. But I do this sort of thing all the time."

"Do what sort of thing? Was that bungee-jumping, what we were doing?"

"Not exactly. If I'd been an ordinary bungee-jumper I should have tied an old towel round my ankles, attached the line and gone down head-first. My weight would have been calculated to the nearest ounce in order to get the line accurate to the nearest inch, so picking up an extra seven or eight stone on the way could have given each of us an extremely nasty headache."

"Then what . . . ?"

"An invention of my own. Hasn't got a name yet. 'Bungeetwist' might do. I wear the sort of harness that bridge-swingers use, but with a swivel clip. I go down feet first, as we did yesterday. The idea is to do as many spiral turns and somersaults and flying movements as possible while I'm bouncing up and down, before coming to rest. When I've worked out a perfect routine I shall apply to have it included in the Olympics, while I'm still the only person who can do it. So you see, taking a passenger on board was no big deal."

"The extra weight, though, as you said . . ."

"That's what a Dangerous Sports player needs, just a touch of actual danger, otherwise it all becomes too predictable. Although really none of these things is as dangerous as crossing the road. It's all in the mind. Anyway, I'm clearly not in your league for danger. No one's ever tried to toss me off a bridge. What was going on?"

I started to tell him, but was interrupted by Mum's return. Pausing only to discover his real name, which

102

was Brian Rogers, and to introduce them, I asked about the news from The Millstone.

"Rufus Fergie phoned about an hour ago. He told Janet he was on the move, so he couldn't leave a number, but he would phone again at two o'clock this afternoon."

"Then I've got to be there." I was angry with Rufus for making contact so difficult, since Janet would certainly have told him how urgent it was that we should speak. "Mum, my car will have been towed away somewhere. Could you get hold of a hire car?"

"Darling you can't possibly—"

"Yes, I can. I mean, I can't drive, but I can leave, if you'll be chauffeur. I'm beautifully strapped up and you can check me in at the John Radcliffe as soon as I've taken the call, if you like." Headington, rising from swampy Oxford to the dizzy height of at least three hundred feet, is home to a cluster of hospitals, all within crawling distance of The Millstone. "Can you find my clothes and bag anywhere?"

Stupid question! My clothes would be caked with mud and my bag, I realised even as I spoke, had been abandoned in the Renault. I would need to cancel credit cards, change locks – damn. All that, though, would have to wait.

"Hold it!" said Bodger. "I have a car. I'd be delighted to drive you both to Oxford. That will be easy. Getting out of here may be more difficult. Just hang on while I park in a getaway position."

He was gone for about ten minutes. I used the time to listen to Mum's story.

"I don't really understand what happened," she said. "The hotel ordered a taxi for us. I was a bit surprised when it was a minicab which turned up, but I told him where to go and got in. Mayuko was just about to follow when she muttered something about needing to check for

103

a message, slammed the car door and ran back inside. I was a bit put out, I must say. It wasn't as if anyone knew where we were, except you."

And Rufus, I thought, remembering what the hotel receptionist had told me, but I didn't interrupt.

"We were actually in good time for the train, so I didn't chase after her. But then suddenly the cab driver took off. He obviously assumed, when he heard the door slam, that Mayuko was inside with me. When I told him to stop and go back, he just went faster."

"So you don't actually know for sure what happened to Mayuko? I mean, she could have been running away again."

"I suppose that's possible." Mum's voice was doubtful. "But why? I mean, she can't have been in league with the driver. And what possible reason could she have for trying to get me out of the way?"

"She phoned Rufus from that hotel," I said thoughtfully. "It all comes back to Rufus. I really must be there to take his call. He's got a great deal of explaining to do."

The curtains of my cubicle were drawn aside with a flourish intended to make it clear that there was nothing underhand about what was to happen next – which there was. The amazing Bodger had somehow taken possession of a porter's coat and a wheelchair.

"X-ray," he said to the young nurse who came to see what was going on; and she believed him enough to provide a blanket to cover my legs. No doubt I could have discharged myself without playing this charade, but the process would have taken time which I couldn't spare.

While we waited for the lift, Bodger ran his fingers up and down my bare spine in a most unprofessional manner between the tapes which tied the hospital's shroud-like garment at the back. I found the touch of his fingertips as exciting as his life-saving embrace had been on the previous evening. "Stop it!" I said huskily, but was glad when he airily ignored the order.

Down at ground level I was wheeled briskly in the direction of the X-ray department and equally briskly out of a side door.

"Into the back," Bodger suggested. "You'll find a lap belt more comfortable than a diagonal." He had already pushed the front passenger seat as far forward as it would go. Mum got in beside me and we drove off.

I might have expected Bodger to be a reckless driver, but consideration for my tender spots held him in check. There were no swerves, no sudden brakings. Only when we reached the motorway did he put on speed – and even then was careful not to exceed the limit. The more I saw of Bodger, the more I liked him.

"Shouldn't you be working?" I asked.

He shook his head. "I finished at university at the end of June. Did without a gap year between school and university, so I reckon I'm entitled to a few months of glorious freedom now. Which is the positive-thinking way of saying that I haven't yet managed to find a job."

"So you're spending your time jumping off bridges!"

"That sort of thing. And catching people who throw other people off bridges. I hope you're going to let me help. I fancy myself as a private detective."

It was true that I was in no state to do much in that line myself, but I didn't say anything to accept the offer. There were dangers and dangers. Instead, I asked him why he was called Bodger.

"Natural elision from Brian to Rogers. Anyway, that's my story. My mother puts it differently. When I was a kid I always managed to mess things up. Paint a picture and then spill water all over it. Clean the car and leave a great patch of dirt somewhere. Put up shelves with screws just a little bit too short. It was my mother who started using the name, and it stuck. Mothers are awful that way, aren't they?"

"I call Kit 'Kitten'," said Mum helpfully.

"Thank you very much!" I bared my teeth at her in mock rage. "That's supposed to be a secret."

"I won't tell anyone, Kitten," Bodger said happily – and then won my heart even more completely by realising that I was too tired to talk. Steadily and in silence he drove along the M4, turned off on to the A34, negotiated three separate sets of road works, took the ring road round the south and east of Oxford and there we were.

Maggie's eyes widened in horror when she saw me being helped inside. Mum tapped out a message of reassurance that my own fingers couldn't manage and then came upstairs to help me dress. There was an hour and a half to wait for the phone call, so as soon as the class broke up for lunch I had time to ask how Janet was getting on. The tuition was going well, she reported; but I was alarmed to hear that Mr Tanaka of the Japanese embassy had phoned. Had he got wind of the kidnapping? Perhaps the family had received a ransom note. She'd promised that I would call back; but that could wait until after I'd spoken to Rufus.

In spite of my wobbly state, I joined the others in the dining room for lunch, to show that I hadn't deserted them. Although my right hand wasn't completely useless, I allowed Maggie to feed me like a baby. She loved it. This was a day when I had to be grateful to her for a change.

Rufus phoned on the stroke of two. Well, that was something; but it didn't stop me from pitching straight in as soon as Mum had propped up the receiver so that I could both hear and speak without touching it.

"Rufus, I really must be able to keep in touch with you. So much has been happening here. It's important—"

"Steady down, Kit. Yes, I know, and I'm sorry. There

106

have been complications. And a new one today. Did you hear the news this morning?"

This was not the time to explain just why I had been in no position to listen to news bulletins recently. "No."

"Mayuko's grandfather has died."

"Does that rate the British news?"

"Well, he's one of the richest men in the world. And it sent the Japanese stock exchange into a dive. Anyway, the thing is, of course Mayuko will have to fly back at once. Her uncle's on his way to fetch her now."

I took a deep breath. This was the moment for confession. "I don't know where she is, Rufus."

I expected him to be incredulous and furious. Instead, he said lightly, "That's all right. Mayuko's with me."

"She's what!" I was the one to be incredulous and furious. "Are you telling me you've known all the time . . . ?" I found myself spluttering incoherently, and he interrupted before I could tell him what I thought of someone who had let me get very nearly murdered for lack of some basic information.

"I said I was sorry, Kit, and I am. Things haven't worked out quite as I'd hoped. I realise I've got a lot of explaining to do. I'll be with you – we'll both be with you – at four o'clock, OK? Straighten the whole thing out. Make sure that we're both telling the same story if anyone starts asking questions."

"But look—"

"Four o'clock," he repeated; and rang off.

"I – am – so – angry!" I shouted, giving each syllable its full weight as Mum put the receiver back. "It's lucky for Mr Rufus Fergie that my fingers aren't up to strangling anyone today. Did you hear that?"

"Yes. I don't think much of it myself. I shall be interested to hear whose idea those handcuffs were."

"I could do some strangling for you," Bodger offered

107

cheerfully. "It's my chance to get a rival out of the way. Although to judge by your expression you're rather less than madly in love with him at the moment."

To calm myself down, I got him to put through a call to Sasha. As I'd feared, my reception was prickly.

"You didn't come," he accused. "I waited one hour ten minutes and you didn't come."

"I never reached London at all. I had an accident and spent the night in hospital." That was all true, although hardly the whole truth. "I felt awful about letting you down, but there was no way—"

"An accident! Are you badly hurt? Are you still in hospital?"

"No, I just got home. Covered in bandages but not too bad."

"I shall come and see you," he said. "Tonight, after work."

I was on the point of telling him not to bother, but remembered just in time that only twenty-four hours earlier it had seemed vital to have a chat with him. In all the recent excitement, I had forgotten about Tilda.

The reminder left me in a sombre mood and I was still brooding on it when Mort paid an unexpected visit.

"Thought I'd better pop in and warn you unofficially, Kit my love," he said in his old-fashioned fatherly-policeman voice. "People are asking questions about you. Want to know about your character. Can you be trusted? Do you play jokes? There'll be two detectives from Bristol arriving soon to take a statement, and they're pretending to be not best pleased at having to make the journey. As if anyone wouldn't be glad of a free jaunt to Oxford! There was something about committing suicide and stealing an NHS nightdress. I don't know which they regard as the more serious. I presume there's something else behind it."

"Miss Quilter is suffering the effects of concussion, as well as her more obvious injuries." Bodger had slipped out of the way at the sight of a uniformed policeman, but now reappeared wearing a white doctor's coat from my role play cupboard. "As with any head injury patient, she's not altogether responsible for her actions at the moment. What she needs is a period of absolute rest, without any stimulation or pressure."

"Then you'd better prescribe that she gets back into that nightdress and goes to bed." Mort wasn't fooled for a moment. "They'll be here about five, I reckon. Just thought I'd let you know, Kit my love."

"Thanks, Mort." I took a deep breath as he left, and thought to myself that Bodger's prescription might not be far off the mark. Too many unanswered questions were fighting for space in my mind. There was the mystery of Mayuko, even though it now appeared that she had run away to be with Rufus rather than being kidnapped; and there was the murder of Tilda. Well, at least Mort hadn't brought the Oxford rapist back into the puzzle again.

Mum was as much in need of a rest as I was, and her car was still where she had left it in the drive two days earlier. In gratitude for his life-saving activities she had invited Bodger to stay and explore Oxford for a day or two, so they moved off in convoy. I hoped he wouldn't repay her hospitality by parachuting from the top of Magdalen tower.

There was an hour and a half left to wait until four o'clock. I used some of the time to give Radhika a one-to-one tutorial in study skills, but the rest of the time passed slowly, allowing my anger to sizzle and my plastered fingers to throb. At least Rufus had solved one problem for me. There was no further need for me to press the police to search for Mayuko. Since Mum had reported her missing, that meant yet another apology to add to any necessary grovelling on the subject of running away from hospital.

In order to take my mind off everything else, I joined Janet's conversation class and allowed myself to be interviewed about the way I'd reached my present sorry state. While the others asked questions Radhika took hold of my right hand. The compress had come away, allowing a fine display of black, blue and purple. The touch was painful for the first few seconds, but then her gentle massage began to rub away the pain. It must be true that there was nothing broken. I began to flex my fingers as I talked and listened. The first movement needed willpower, but before long it became possible to believe that I should soon be able to hold things again.

All the time, though, I was listening for the sound of the bell. At five to four I asked Louise to open the front door for me; and as she did so the sound of a car could be heard coming up the drive.

It drew to a halt and Rufus got out: even taller than I remembered him, and looking older than a man who, like me, was still under thirty. He went round to open the passenger door.

I stared uncomprehendingly. His passenger was female. She was Japanese. But she was not Mayuko.

Chapter Nine

I'd intended to stride out with all guns blazing, to make sure that Rufus and Mayuko both realised how inconsiderate they'd been; but the sight of a stranger checked me before I began. And she was not the only unexpected visitor. From the back seat of the car out stepped a man with a camera. He snapped the Japanese girl as she looked up at The Millstone and snapped her again as she advanced towards me with outstretched hand. The camera remained in shooting position as he waited for me to smile in welcome; but I let him wait.

Rufus approached me with an uncertain expression on his face, as well he might. Probably he didn't know whether to shake hands or kiss. I was wearing a loose jacket over my shoulders, and shook it open enough to show some of my bandages.

"What have you done to yourself?" he asked, concerned; but I was not interested in giving him an account of my state of health.

"Where's Mayuko?" I demanded instead.

"Here she is."

"Don't play games with me, Rufus."

"I told you I had a lot of explaining to do. A lot of apologising, as well. Can we go inside?"

"Not until you've told me what this is all about."

He sighed as he performed an introduction. "Kit, this is May. Mayuko. May, meet Kit Quilter."

She smiled, and held out a hand for a second time, although she could see that I wasn't going to take it. "I'm very pleased to meet you, Miss Quilter." The camera whirred again.

"No photographs, you told me, Rufus. Specifically, no photographs."

"That was then, when you were teaching an impostor. This is now, when you're meeting the real thing." He led the way inside the house.

It was teatime, but I wasn't feeling hospitable. Janet and the group would be sitting round the table on the terrace now, and afterwards would return to the billiards room. I led my visitors into the drawing room.

"If this is Mayuko, who have I been teaching?" This was no time for correct grammar.

"Her name is Hiromi." It was May who answered. "She is schoolfriend of mine, and not to blame in this. Mr Fergie, will you leave me with Miss Quilter for a moment, please? I am the one who must make apologies."

That use of 'Mr Fergie' startled me slightly; perhaps only because everyone in England seems to be on Christian name terms with everyone else these days. My rage reduced from boiling point to simmering as I stared at the poised young woman who faced me across the room.

Expensively and stylishly dressed, and with her sleek hair elaborately coiled into a chignon, May looked exactly as I had originally expected my rich young pupil to look. Unlike – what was her name, Hiromi? – unlike Hiromi, she was self-confident, even sophisticated. Well, perhaps Hiromi had been sophisticated as well, and had merely put on a mumbling act of shyness. It also appeared that today's arrival had a much better command of English than her friend – and the confidence to speak it. As Rufus left the room, she leaned forward slightly on the sofa.

112

"Mr Fergie has told you, perhaps, that I am to be married soon?"

I nodded.

"This marriage is my duty, and I shall do my duty to my family. I shall have much honour, and much happiness, I am sure. Except that my father and mother died together long ago, I have been most fortunate in my circumstances. But always until now I have lived in my uncle's house and under his discipline; and soon I shall be with my husband and obedient to him. That is expected." She faltered for a moment, and then repeated, "I am most fortunate. But I said to Mr Fergie, one day when he came to give a lesson to my cousin, that I would very much like to be free for a little while. A month, or a week, even. To see something of the world through my own eyes, not my husband's. Do you understand this?"

"Yes." To say that I understood did not necessarily imply that I sympathised. I too had wanted to see the world and had been restrained by duty. Unlike this high-born heiress, though, I had not tried to escape from Maggie. "You say you are to blame, but you can't have planned this yourself."

"No." She bowed her head in agreement. "No, it was Mr Fergie who made the first suggestion that I should come to England to improve my English. And I thought it was to be as it was arranged, that you would teach me and I would see Oxford and London and a play of William Shakespeare at Stratford and make friends with your other pupils. And in doing all that I would feel free. But I found that you or your mother would always be with me; and my Uncle Shin would require a bodyguard to watch at night. So then I was not quite so happy. But—" She threw out her hands in a gesture which indicated that she had accepted the restrictions.

"How did it all change?"

"Mr Fergie made the suggestion – to me only – that someone else should take my place on your course. So that I could travel with no one to know where I was. He promised to help me himself. We could go to Paris as well as to London, he said. I have always wanted to visit Paris. I have much interest in fashion design. He told me that my English was already good, and he would talk with me and teach me, so that I should be learning just as my uncle expected. He made it sound very easy."

"And what was Rufus – Mr Fergie – expecting to get out of this?"

"At first I believed he was thinking only of my happiness. Then when we came to Paris he told me that for two years he had loved me, and had waited only until I was older before telling me."

"How did he come to know you?"

"My cousin is not very clever and does badly at school. There are teachers in several subjects who come to the house to give him extra lessons. Mr Fergie is one of these teachers. Sometimes my aunt gives him tea, and I am there. But I did not know of his feelings." She paused, leaving me to imagine the scene which must have taken place in Paris. "He hoped, I think, to free me from the marriage which has been arranged. But this is impossible. I have told him that I must do what I have promised."

"So he tried to seduce you?" This was Rufus running true to form.

A faint flush coloured May's pale cheeks. "He would have liked . . . He told me that in this way also I could have freedom for a little while and no one would ever know. He doesn't understand." The flush deepened. "Before my marriage a doctor must say that I am healthy and can have children – and . . ."

I could hardly control a smile. Mum had not been so far from the mark, then, in suggesting that I ought to demand

114

a certificate of virginity when I took delivery of my pupil. Anyway, I was pleased to hear that Rufus's little plot had ended in frustration.

It seemed to me that the whole idea had been crazy. But a young girl who had never left home before might not have realised what she was getting into; and if Rufus had seriously set his sights on marrying her, the ruin of her reputation could have been to his advantage. It seemed obvious that he was only after her money, and her family would no doubt have paid him handsomely to keep the escapade quiet and save the family's face.

"The death of my grandfather has made everything different," said May. "He was my father's father, and his fortune comes to me. The newspapers write about me for the first time. Now my uncle is flying from Japan to take me home."

"I see." And I did see. "He'll come here to collect you. And he'll expect me to tell him what a studious, dutiful pupil you have been. When I could say that I have been tricked and lied to – and assaulted as well, through your fault." My anger, which had been put on hold, began to bubble again. "I haven't had time to tell you yet about all the trouble which has been caused by this deception. I could have been killed. My mother, too. And as for Hiromi—"

May stood up to face me. Then, very slowly, very deliberately, she sank on to her knees and bowed her head right down to the ground, her hands pressed together in a gesture of submission.

"I have behaved very badly to you, Miss Quilter," she said. "And for myself, very foolishly. I make my apologies to you. I am sorry, I am sorry, I am sorry. If you wish to punish me, you must do so. But I hope . . . I hope . . ." She raised her hands to her face in an effort to conceal the fact that she was crying. "I am very sorry," she said again.

I'm a softie at heart, and the tears had an effect. They were genuine, not pretended tears. Nor did it appear that she was acting under instructions from Rufus about the best way to manipulate me. Rufus would have blustered – indeed, he probably still would try to excuse himself when it was his turn to face me. But it was important to remember that most of my fury and anxiety – and pain – had been caused by Hiromi's disappearance, and May could not be blamed for that. I was looking at a girl who was still young and had probably led an over-protected life. She had made a mistake, as young girls very often do. I'd made the same mistake myself, at much the same age, in choosing to trust Rufus; but it had been possible, although painful, to escape from it undamaged. May's mistake, if I chose to be spiteful, could spoil the rest of her life.

Or, of course, could offer her an escape. That was something to check.

"This marriage which your family has arranged. Is it your own wish? You will be a rich young woman in your own right. You could enjoy the freedom you dreamed about."

She was still on her knees, but raised her head to look at me.

"It is my wish. The shame would be very great if . . . if . . ."

"Sit down again," I said. My bruised hand was too tender to help her up from the floor. I waited until she was comfortable and staring at me anxiously. "Well, now. Telling lies is not something I enjoy. Especially the kind of lies which are liable to be found out. But no one will learn from me anything which you wish to keep secret. I will refuse to answer questions which will make things difficult for you. I will give you now one lesson in English so that it will be true that I have taught you. And you may

116

bring in that photographer." I could understand now why Rufus had thought it important to bring him along.

"Oh, Miss Quilter!" Her eyes brightened, and I think she would have hugged me had it not been for the bandages.

"First of all, though, I want you to answer one or two questions for me. Did you ever meet, in Japan, a friend of Mr Fergie's called Tilda Grace?"

Her puzzled look was perhaps caused as much by the change of subject as by the actual question, because once she had adjusted her mind to it she nodded her head without more hesitation.

"Yes, I remember her, though she didn't stay a very long time. Mr Fergie said to my aunt that it would be good for me to have English conversation. I wasn't weak in the examinations, like my cousin, but I could not speak as well as I could write. He would have liked to make this conversation himself, but my aunt said it was more correct that a lady should teach me. So he gave the name of Miss Grace. But she came only six, seven times and then she went away."

"And Hiromi? Did Hiromi know her as well?"

"Yes. Miss Grace said that it was better to have two than one, and Hiromi was my best friend, so she came to my house for the conversations."

That explained a lot: not the second disappearance, from Bristol, but the dash for the coach in Oxford. No wonder Hiromi was alarmed when she learned that Tilda was due to arrive at The Millstone. She would have phoned Rufus, who undoubtedly told her to keep out of the way for twenty-four hours. Now it was time for me to find out whether Rufus had done anything more than give advice. It would have been as important for him as for the real Mayuko that the imposture should not be discovered.

117

"I have another question to ask you. Think back two days, please. Wednesday morning. Will you tell me everything that happened on Wednesday morning?"

Again she looked puzzled but seemed anxious to be helpful.

"I was in London; the first day after Paris. I had breakfast in the hotel, and then—"

"What time? And did you have it alone?"

"What the hell is going on?" I hadn't noticed Rufus coming into the room. "I don't see what this inquisition has got to do with anything. You sound as though you're trying to play detective."

"And so I am. And I want to hear May's answer before I compare it with yours. Please go outside the house, Rufus. You can tell the photographer that he may come inside."

His face was sulky, but he did what he was told. It gave me a shameful kind of pleasure to hear myself bossing him around. Back in our college days I was the one who had danced to his tune – and had been left to cry when the music ended. Before I allowed May to answer any more questions I asked her to open the door for a second to make sure that he wasn't lingering within earshot.

"Breakfast on Wednesday," I reminded her after she had returned to the sofa.

"I had breakfast at eight o'clock, with Mr Fergie. We had agreed to meet at this time. Afterwards, we went to Harrods. We walked, because it was very close. But we were too early. Mr Fergie made a mistake about the time of opening. So we took a taxi for an hour and saw Buckingham Palace and the column of Nelson and the Houses of Parliament and Westminster Abbey and then returned again to Harrods and it was open. I bought presents for my family."

"And Mr Fergie was with you all that time?"

"Oh yes. All that day and every day. Only at night he was not."

That would seem to absolve him of any involvement in Tilda's murder, although I was set on going through the motions of checking the story with him separately.

"Thank you, May. So! Would you like to come this way?"

I led the way into the billiards room, nodding permission for the photographer to follow. Janet and the others were still having tea, so I was able to give a quick introduction to all my apparatus without wasting time on explanations to them.

May was photographed wearing headphones and listening earnestly to a tape. She was photographed writing in a workbook. She was photographed making a speech while I shot the scene on video. And after she had been invited to take her pick of clothes from the role play cupboard she was photographed in the doctor's white coat which Bodger had recently discarded, with stethoscope hanging round her neck.

"Now I'm going to give you a quick lesson," I said as I had promised. I sat down in between a large mirror and an epidiascope screen and told her to set a chair where she could see both my mouth and hers. "You speak English very well. Very well indeed. But one thing you need to practise is how to say 'Please'."

'Please' is a problem for all Japanese, who find it hard enough to pronounce the letter 'l' even at the beginning of a word and almost impossible when it's tucked away. But it's a problem which I've solved before. I flashed up pictures to show exactly where her tongue should be behind her teeth, and then produced one of my favourite teaching aids: a skull, complete with moving jawbone, into which I've fixed a floppy red tongue which can be moved by hand into the right position at every stage of

119

the word. The photographer went for the skull in a big way, and flashed away non-stop. May, for her part, was as determined as I was that she should succeed quickly and repeated the word over and over again until it was perfect.

"Very good!" I exclaimed truthfully at last. I had intended to move her on through a list of similar problem words, but the very first of them – 'police' – reminded me that I had some more awkward interviews to come, and the stress of the day was beginning to catch up with me. I was glad to be interrupted by the telephone.

Janet came hurrying to take the call, but by now my hand was just about capable of lifting the receiver. The caller was Mr Tanaka.

"I left a message that you must call me back, but you have not done so," he said. "I have just met Mr Nakagami at Heathrow. We are coming directly to your institution." He rang off without inviting comments.

Heathrow to Headington is forty-five minutes on a good day, but rush-hour traffic at half-past four on a summer Friday could easily double that. It would be inconvenient if their arrival coincided with that of the Bristol police.

"Is Mr Nakagami your uncle?" I asked May.

"Yes. My mother's brother."

"Does he speak or understand English?"

"No, not at all."

That was a relief, but one problem remained. "He'll be here in about an hour, and someone from the embassy is with him. The same man who brought Hiromi here, thinking she was you."

"I know what to do. Excuse me, please." Her 'please' was perfect.

The photographer went out with her, giving me a chance to speak to Rufus alone at last. I took him back into the drawing room.

"You're being very decent about all this, Kit. Thanks a lot."

"I'm sorry for her. But there's someone else I'm more sorry for. You don't seem to realise at all what a mess you've got Hiromi into."

"She can stay here till the end of the month and fly back to Japan under her own name. She's enjoying the course immensely. She thinks you're a terrific teacher."

"You're not with me, Rufus. I keep trying to tell you, but you don't seem to be able to understand. She's disappeared. We ought to have every policeman in England looking for her at this moment, but just when I was about to push for the search to be stepped up, you told me Mayuko was with you. You must have realised that to use that name for someone I'd never met would cause a misunderstanding."

"You're being too hard on me, Kit, and there's nothing to worry about. I told Hiromi—"

"Let's go through it one stage at a time," I suggested. His look of pained innocence was beginning to rile me more than somewhat. "The girl I thought was Mayuko phoned to tell you that Tilda was coming here and might recognise her."

"Right. But only coming for one night, it appeared. So yes, I told Hiromi to make herself scarce for twenty-four hours. I'm sorry that you were worried. But—"

"You're not sorry at all. You didn't consider my feelings at any point in this masquerade. Anyway, Hiromi took off for Bristol. What happened next?"

"She phoned again the next morning to say that your mother had gone with her and was about to take her back to Oxford, and would that be all right? I told her yes, fine, and then she called again five minutes' later. She sounded very upset. Said your mother had driven off without her. I said that Lady Quilter was probably fed up about being kept waiting and Hiromi had better make her own way to the station as fast as possible. That's the last contact we had. I was expecting to find her here and ask her to keep out of sight for an hour or so."

"She was kidnapped," I told him bluntly. "So was my mother. The reason Mum was driven off so fast was that the car wasn't a taxi at all. The driver thought he'd got Hiromi as well, and was put out to find that he hadn't. But there must have been a back-up car just behind which picked her up when she came out again. And that's why you *really* ought to be sorry, Rufus. Not just for playing me up, but for the mess you've got Hiromi into. She must be terrified, poor girl, and thanks to you I doubt whether anyone's seriously looking for her. The police will be here in less than an hour, and they'll have to know the truth."

"The police? You could tell them—"

"Oh yes!" I flared up. "There are all sorts of things I could tell them, but why should I? Why do you expect me to make a liar of myself to get all *your* chestnuts out of the fire. If you'd only thought sensibly for a moment before you started this ridiculous business—"

"I was in love with her," said Rufus. "With May. I've been in love with her for more than two years, ever since . . . Waiting for her to grow up. Hoping that she'd love me and have the strength to break away. It wasn't just the money. It was meeting her while she was still a child and watching her change to a woman, still so sweet and obedient and uncorrupted. It's been so lonely, Kit. Eight years. I hoped I'd found someone to love me at last."

Did he think I'd believe that? Calmer now, I stared at him as though he was a stranger. Ten years earlier he had been more than handsome. Intelligence and a love of adventure had put a sparkle in his eyes; his skin had been silky with the ruddy health of youth; he was energetic

122

and full of life. Now there was something seedy about him. The pallor of a polluted city had replaced that of a prison and there were deep lines not only across his forehead but down from the corners of his mouth. His shining golden hair had faded to a stringy yellow. His eyes no longer met mine in shared laughter, but flickered furtively away. He was too thin and, instead of carrying his height proudly, had begun to stoop at the shoulders. It was as if the stuffing had gone out of him. Well, he had had more than his share of rotten luck, and perhaps there were not many people who would have taken all that on the chin and come up smiling.

"Anyway," he said now. "That's all behind me. I've made a fool of myself in more ways than one. I ought to have guessed . . . More wasted years! Girls can be very selfish, can't they?"

It was tempting to tell him exactly what I thought of that remark! But something in his hangdog expression had got through to me. He'd treated me badly once, but I'd survived. I could afford to be sorry for someone who found himself stuck up to the neck in despond. I'd meant to push the responsibility for rescuing Hiromi firmly on to his shoulders, but it was obvious that they weren't broad enough to carry the burden.

"Why were you asking May all those questions?" he said abruptly. It reminded me that I wanted to put the same questions to him – and hoped to receive the same answers. He gave them, which was a relief. Unless there was a deeper conspiracy than seemed likely, he couldn't have been at Oxford to kill Tilda. Only then did it occur to me that he might not know about her death.

I didn't tell him directly. There was one more question to be asked, although probably Rufus would find it impertinent. It might prove to be irrelevant; but equally it might have some bearing on the reason for her death.

"Will you tell me, Rufus," I asked, "what exactly happened between you and Tilda to make her leave Japan?"

Chapter Ten

Rufus was taken aback by my question. "I don't see what business it is—"

"I'm not just being nosy. I've got a reason for asking. I'll tell you in a minute."

He still wasn't sure, and gave me an odd look. Perhaps he was remembering how he'd ditched me for Tilda all those years ago and wondering whether I was probing out of an old jealousy. But my expression was serious, and in the end he gave me a serious answer.

"When I went off to Libya, we were very much in love, Tilda and I," he said. "It wasn't easy, spending a year apart, but when you know an end date you can make it tolerable. But then there was the prison thing. At first I thought every day, every week, must surely be the last. I couldn't believe . . . There wasn't even a trial. After a bit, of course, it swung the other way. There seemed no reason why it should ever end. The only thing that kept me sane was the thought of Tilda slogging away on my behalf, pestering people. She wrote me letters. Only about one a year got through, but she put numbers on them, so I could know she was thinking of me more often than it seemed."

It was best not to make any comment on this. I knew about those numbers. Tilda had confessed once how appalled she'd been to realise that six months had passed since her last letter, and how she proposed to conceal the fact.

"I realised, of course, that she'd have to get on with earning a living. But I hoped . . . I didn't have anyone but her to dream about, you see, while I was shut up there. Fantasies. An imaginary woman. While she had real men. I ought to have realised. If it had been you, Kit, you'd have stuck by me, wouldn't you?"

I wasn't going to answer that one. There might once have been a moment when I'd hoped that Rufus would transfer his affections back to me, but that moment was long past.

"Well then, I got out at last. It took me a little while to track her down, because she was doing a temporary job that she hadn't known about when she last wrote. I found her in the end, just before I was due to take up a job in Japan."

Knowing this already, I waited patiently.

"It all seemed marvellous. Just what I'd hoped for. She was happy to see me, happy to come with me. I wasn't much good in bed for the first few weeks and she was sympathetic about that as well until it came right. I thought it was all going to be happy-ever-after stuff. Until one day I discovered that she'd made an appointment to have an abortion."

"Your baby?"

"I took that for granted at first, although it seemed a bit early for her to know that she was pregnant. We had a row, but it was only half a row. I was angry with her for trying to go behind my back. But pleased at the same time, about there being a baby, I mean, because I was ready to get married, start a family. That was when she told me that the baby wasn't mine. She'd thought of pretending that it was, she said, but quite apart from the timing problem, she'd decided it wouldn't be fair. That was what got me, Kit. You wouldn't believe the smugness of it! I was supposed to believe that she was behaving so

126

perfectly in not fobbing off someone else's kid on me. Didn't even seem to occur to her that there were other ways of behaving well, like waiting, keeping herself."

"Five years, Rufus. It was a very long time. You couldn't really expect—"

"Yes, I bloody well could!" he shouted. There was a moment in which he seemed to be re-living the rage he had felt then. "I hit her. I've never hit a woman before. Or since. I really beat her up." He laughed without amusement. "It saved her the cost of the abortion, as things turned out. She was lucky, if she only knew it. I could have killed her."

"Then it's just as well you have a good alibi for Wednesday morning."

"What's that supposed to mean?"

"I mean that Tilda is dead, Rufus. Murdered."

He stared at me as though he couldn't believe what he'd heard. I knew the feeling.

"The police think that it was an attempted rape that went wrong. I don't go along with that theory myself. It leaves too many questions unanswered. You might try thinking back on any conversations which could suggest a motive, a possible murderer."

"It's more than two years since I last spoke to her." He was still dazed – or seemed to be. "Tilda, dead!"

The conversation was interrupted by a sound which was rasping in our ear-drums. Noise from the air is a familiar nuisance to me, for The Millstone is inside the circle which a police helicopter uses to keep an eye on the crowds coming to watch Oxford United's home matches, to my fortnightly annoyance. But this was so much louder, and approaching so fast, that for a moment I thought it was going to crash.

But no, it was simply landing in my garden. You'd think that as a matter of politeness, if not of law, people should ask permission before blowing over other people's regale lilies. I was not well pleased as I hurried outside to see what was happening.

Mr Tanaka was the first to climb down, followed by an older man with shiny black hair and shiny black shoes. He was so small that he didn't feel any need to duck as he walked under the rotor blades towards the house. From the imperious way in which he gestured to Mr Tanaka to stay behind, I deduced that he was Uncle Shin. I ought to have guessed that Uncle Shin was not likely to expose himself to the M25 in the rush hour.

His niece appeared from the front of the house. She had presumably been dipping into her luggage, which was still in Rufus's car. I had to give her full marks for forethought. Over her summer dress she was wearing a long black silk coat and on her head was a black hat with an opaque mourning veil. I'd never seen anything like it outside a royal funeral and stared in fascination as she exchanged bows. There was no danger of Mr Tanaka challenging her as an impostor, as I'd feared.

Speaking in Japanese, she introduced her uncle to me. Not being well up in the etiquette of degrees of bowing, I inclined my head politely. After that he made a short but incomprehensible speech before signalling his companion to fetch something from the helicopter.

"I am to go back with him at once," said May. "But first he would like to make a gift to you, in thanks for your work. And also to the other young ladies, my new friends, with whom I have been studying." She looked worried about this, as well she might.

The rest of the group had all rushed round from the terrace to see what was going on – alarmed at first, like me, by the sound of the helicopter's engine. Taking advantage of Uncle Shin's lack of English, I thanked him with smiles for the handsome gold bracelet which he handed to me, and then turned to the others and produced a hasty story.

"You're about to be given a present by the uncle of someone who has been one of my pupils. He thinks that you're all her friends and doesn't realise that my groups change so frequently. I suggest you simply accept what he offers without trying to straighten it out."

In exchange for this advice I received five grins of complicity. Only Radhika was uncertain what was going on, and waited until last so that she could watch how the others reacted. When her turn came, Uncle Shin looked from her to Nonny – the African model – and back again before handing over the gift-wrapped box, and asked a question.

"My uncle expected that all my companions would be English," May translated. The comment didn't give me a very high opinion of his intelligence.

"Explain to him that English girls don't need to learn English. Each one of my pupils comes from a different country, to make sure that English is the only language they have in common. And then ask him if he wishes to see the house." Since Uncle Shin was paying the bill, it seemed only fair for him to see what his money had bought.

He looked at his watch before accepting, and nodded with apparent approval at the apparatus on display. There was another question. "He would like to see the room in which I slept."

"Then you will have to remind him that you spent every night in the house of Lady Quilter, my mother, in order that you should be well chaperoned."

"Yes, of course."

The tour ended. May's luggage was brought round from Rufus's car and loaded aboard. A sudden flash of inspiration prompted me to send Janet in search of my camera. All the photographs taken earlier in the afternoon would undoubtedly go back to Japan, as a record of the visit to England. I could think of uses for a few snaps of my own. Facing away from Mr Tanaka, Mayuko temporarily threw back her veil for Janet to photograph her with the helicopter in the background. While she adjusted her camouflage, I returned to the waiting group for a quiet word with Mr Tanaka.

"You hired a bodyguard who turned out to be a crook. There will be criminal charges. I'm expecting the police here within the next half-hour to take details. Will you tell me, please, the name of the agency you used and give me the man's full name and address?"

"I told you before on the telephone, it was at Mr Nakagami's request that this arrangement was made, because he saw news reports of attacks on young women in Oxford."

"But you were the one who actually made the arrangement. And you picked a wrong 'un."

"I cannot believe—"

But at that moment, by happy but not unexpected chance, two plain clothes police, one male and one female, appeared on the lawn after failing to get any answer from the front door bell. Had there been any danger – and thanks to the veil, there was not – of Mr Tanaka pausing to check whether the young lady just leaving The Millstone was the same as the one he had earlier brought there, it disappeared promptly as he fished a notebook from his pocket and copied out an entry.

"The man's address I do not know, but the agency will tell you."

"Thank you very much. Goodbye then, Mayuko."

"Goodbye, Miss Quilter. And thank you so very much for all you have done. I am so grateful. So sorry, also."

This should have been Rufus's cue to step forward, even though he could hardly have hoped to travel back with the family party. But he stayed out of sight. He had lost her, and no doubt this was a bitter moment for him.

Since my strapped shoulder would allow me to cover only one ear as the helicopter took off, I retreated inside the house, nodding to the police to follow me. It would have been nice to have a breathing space between crises, but obviously that luxury was not on offer. My first plan, after Mort's warning, had been to take refuge in a severe case of amnesia; but that was while I was still under the impression that Rufus was just about to arrive with the girl I had known as Mayuko. Now it had again become urgent to find the kidnap victim, so I would have to do a certain amount of remembering.

Once the noise had subsided, my new visitors introduced themselves as Detective Inspector Carey and Detective Sergeant Wallis, from Bristol. I gave myself a few seconds' thinking time by asking Maggie, in the kitchen, to provide tea and cake for the new arrivals. When I returned to the drawing room I was able without too much exaggeration to give the impression of being only one or two steps from death's door.

"I really must apologise for having put you to the trouble of coming here. I was worried about missing this extremely important meeting with someone who has flown from Japan to speak to me and could only stay very briefly in England. And in any case my mother, Lady Quilter, is the one who can give you first-hand information about the kidnapping. I've only heard the facts indirectly."

"In the first place," said the inspector, with the look of one confronting a murder suspect, "Lady Quilter also disappeared from Bristol before we could interview her properly. And in the second place, we have a few questions to ask about how you came to find yourself at the bottom of the Avon gorge last night."

"Can we leave that for the moment and concentrate on the kidnap, because that's the urgent thing." There was a pause while Maggie handed round tea and chocolate cake, which produced a slight thawing in the atmosphere. "Hiromi is a stranger in our country, her English is not good and she's only eighteen. She'll be terrified."

"Hiromi?" The female detective produced a notebook and frowned into it. "Name given to us was Mayuko, surname unknown. Is Hiromi the surname?"

"No. I expect my mother was as confused by what happened as the kidnappers themselves must be. No doubt she heard them mention the name: the wrong name. The position is this. There are two Japanese girls, who both came to England to learn English. One of them, Mayuko, comes from a very rich family. The other one, Hiromi, well, I don't suppose she's poor, but she's nothing special in the money line. The kidnappers had found out that Mayuko, the rich one, was in England. I presume they hoped to get a huge ransom for her. But when it came to the snatch, they couldn't tell the difference between one Japanese face and another. They took the wrong one. They *think* they've got Mayuko, but actually they're holding Hiromi."

"How do you know?" That was the inspector again, still suspicious.

"Well, Mayuko is safe. We've just this moment waved her goodbye."

"What I mean is, how do you know that the other one has been kidnapped?"

"Because she's missing."

"People go missing voluntarily."

"Not girls like her, in a foreign country. All her possessions are still here. And I'm sure she'd have been in touch with me if she could. Besides, what else would explain the way my mother's been treated?"

"Have you received any ransom note?"

"No, but it wouldn't come to me. They'd write directly to Mayuko's family, wouldn't they? And the trouble is that the family wouldn't know what on earth the message meant, because of course they'd have Mayuko safely sitting there in their midst, so they might well do nothing about it."

"So when do you believe that this young lady," – he glanced down at his notes – "Hiromi, was taken?"

"Yesterday morning."

"Then why has it taken you so long to report it?"

"For God's sake!" But there was no point in getting indignant. "She was staying in Bristol overnight with my mother. I wasn't expecting her back here until yesterday evening, so I had no reason to start worrying until then, when they didn't turn up. If I *had* reported her missing at once, wouldn't I have been told what you've just been trying to say: that I was worrying unnecessarily about someone who'd probably only missed her train?"

"But you were worried enough to travel to Bristol."

"I find it difficult to understand whether you're accusing me of worrying too much or too little," I protested. "My mother managed to get her hands on a portable phone to tell me where she was. I hoped to find the two of them together. When they weren't, and when I was unable to release my mother, I moved as quickly as I could to find a telephone box or a policeman. Unfortunately I was involved in an accident, but the first thing I did when someone found me was to ask him to call the police. And the first thing I told the police was that there had been a kidnapping. That was getting on for twenty-four hours ago. If *I'm* allowed to ask a question now, I'd like to know what you've been doing about it."

"No need to get upset, miss. About this accident, then . . ."

"Can't that wait? I don't actually remember much of what happened. I cracked my head on the windscreen." That much was true, and I pointed to the bruise on my forehead to prove it. "I don't know whether I was thrown out of the car or got out and lost my balance, or what." My memory could make a convenient return when it came to accusing someone of attempted murder. "None of that's as important for me as finding this girl I'm responsible for. I can suggest two ways of tracing the kidnappers."

I passed over the address of the security firm which Mr Tanaka had employed. "There's a chap called Mike, employed by this firm, who was hired to act as a body-guard to the rich girl, Mayuko. My mother recognised him as one of the men who was guarding her. I've seen him and can identify him as well. He's a large, stupid-looking lout." I described his bruiser's face as well as I could. "The agency should be able to put you on his track."

"And you believe he was so stupid that he couldn't distinguish between one girl and another?" This was Sergeant Wallis chipping in again.

"Yes. A lot of people are like that. Well, you must know, from organising identity parades. They think it's enough to identify someone as Japanese, black, bearded or whatever; and so it may be if he's the only one. But when there are two, they find they haven't bothered to look properly. In any case, from what my mother has told me, Mike himself kept out of the way during the actual snatch. He'd got at least two accomplices – and they'd probably never had more than a fleeting glimpse of the girl they wanted." I was remembering the confrontation in the Vicky Arms. Almost certainly that was where the plot was hatched.

"You indicated that there might be some other way in which you could help," the inspector reminded me.

134

I nodded my head towards the camera which Janet had left on a coffee table.

"My fingers aren't in very good working order at the moment, I'm afraid. But if you wind that film right through you can take it away with you. The last couple of shots are of Mayuko, the rich one, on the point of leaving England to go to her grandfather's funeral in Japan. If you give this case a bit of publicity and get some newspapers to print a picture and make it clear that it was taken today, the kidnappers will realise that they've got the wrong girl. With any luck, they'll decide that it isn't worth hanging on to her."

"Right." I had done it. A new briskness in Inspector Carey's voice suggested that he had decided to believe this was a case worth investigating and not the blathering of some nut with concussion. "We shall want a photograph of this girl, Hiromi. And her surname, of course, and whatever details you can give of her." Naturally – but incorrectly – he was assuming that I had all the relevant information in her registration details.

"I wonder if you'd excuse me for a few minutes," I said, getting to my feet and giving a fine display of stagger. "I've got the most killing headache, and I really must lie down for a bit. There's someone else who can tell you—" I had reached the door by now, and called through it. "Rufus!"

He came so quickly that he had probably been eavesdropping at the door. It would make things simpler if he had.

"I've just been explaining about Hiromi being kidnapped in mistake for Mayuko," I murmured. "Could you tell them everything they want to know about Hiromi while I rest up for a little while?"

"Sure." He went in and closed the door behind him, relieving me of the need to continue my act while I made for the telephone in the office. It was Mum whose number I called, but Bodger who answered.

"Bodger, I need Hiromi's passport, for the photograph. Do you think you could find it and bring it up here? She'll have hidden it away so that Mum wouldn't catch sight of it casually, but it must be in her room somewhere."

"Is this a trap to get me into the hands of the law?" he enquired cautiously.

"They're here, certainly. But they won't have the foggiest idea who you are. You can post the passport through the front door and run, if you like."

"If the alternative is that I can take you out to dinner, I'll be very brave and actually ring the bell."

"We shall eat here," I told him. "My table manners aren't up to a restaurant yet. How's my mother?"

"Gone to bed with a sleeping pill. Very wisely. Hence my need for an alternative trough. I'll be with you in ten minutes or so."

I could use that ten minutes to prove to the detectives that I wasn't a liar in claiming that I needed to rest. Getting upstairs was almost too much of an effort, but I made it at last and collapsed on to the bed. Before the first sheep stood up to be counted, I was asleep.

Chapter Eleven

I was awakened by a light kiss on the lips. It felt so delightful that I kept my eyes shut in the hope that it would be repeated. It was.

"You're awake," said Bodger's voice. "I know you're awake and you know that I know."

I smiled happily, pursing my lips up to invite kiss number three before reluctantly opening my eyes.

"Poor battered Sleeping Beauty," he said. "Although I have to confess that a deep purple patch in the middle of the forehead is very fetching. Every woman should have one."

"Have the police gone?"

"Yes. Someone called Rufus handed over the passport and told them you were unfit for further interrogation. He, the Rufus man, seems to think he's staying for supper. Ought I to be jealous of Rufus?"

"No."

"Well, I am. And now somebody else has arrived and is demanding to see you in a wild Russian accent. He calls himself Sasha and *he* seems to think he's staying for supper as well. Ought I to be jealous of Sasha?"

"No. Oh, Christ!" I struggled to sit up. For the second day running I had forgotten all about Sasha.

"Well, I am. Here am I, looking forward to an intimate candlelit dinner, and what do I find? That the room will be crowded with adoring swains, competing for your favours. Also, it's time I was told what is going on here. I mean to say, here am I again, practising to invent a new Dangerous Sport, and I find myself hopelessly outclassed by someone who lets herself be tossed off bridges without even an elastic band to hold on to."

"It was lovely," I said dreamily. "I thought we were going to die together. I almost wanted it, it felt so wonderful."

Bodger helped me to my feet and clasped his arms round my waist, just as he had over the Avon gorge, although not quite as tightly.

"Yes," he said, unexpectedly serious. "It's very important to choose the right company to die in. But I hope we may have a bit of living together first. It's frustrating, not being able to do the Prince Charming act straight away. How are you?"

"My right hand's almost back to normal." It was still black and swollen, but I could use my fingers. "Bodger, of course I shall be happy to tell you about everything that's been going on. But I do need to have a private chat with Sasha at some point in the evening." An idea struck me. Janet would have gone home by now. "Would you be willing to talk to my girls for half an hour or so after dinner? About your Dangerous Sports, perhaps? They'd be fascinated, and it would introduce new vocabulary for them."

"Am I to understand that you're hiring me to give English conversation classes?"

"I'm offering you the chance to flirt with six intelligent young women."

"Flirt? Me?" Laughing, he kissed me again. "Well, all right, I'll chat them up. But don't blame me if they all start jumping off the Whispering Gallery in St Paul's without parachutes. For the moment, I've been sent to tell you that dinner will be ready in ten minutes."

I used part of the ten minutes to welcome Sasha, repeat my apologies about the previous evening, suggest a stroll together after the meal and generally smooth down his ruffled feelings. Then Maggie gave the Chinese gong in the hall a good hammering to summon us all to the dining room; I don't think she realises what a racket it makes.

Dinner was a feast. The prospect of visitors always inspires Maggie, and although Bodger had turned up at short notice, she had had good warning of Sasha's arrival. Very often during the girls' courses their pupil-lessons take the form of cookery classes featuring some national speciality. We all move into the kitchen so that Maggie can watch and remember a practical demonstration, but of course the demonstrator is expected to explain everything aloud as she works, and I act as scribe, writing down quantities. Tonight the menu was international.

We started with a magnificently authentic bouillabaisse: I could have guessed, even if I hadn't known, that it was Louise who had most recently accompanied Maggie on the regular shopping trip to the Covered Market and had helped her to pick the right fish and crustaceans. I was short on appetite, and happy to regard that as my main course, but the others pressed on with venison and an assortment of mushrooms in a rich wine sauce, from a Polish recipe. The market had also, as always, provided good cheeses; and to end the meal Maggie whipped up a creamy zabaglione.

By the time we adjourned to the drawing room for coffee we were all in a blissful mood of gluttonous contentment; except for Rufus, whose face was pale and anxious. Perhaps he looked like that all the time these days; it was the contrast with that happy college photograph which struck me. Was he upset about Tilda's death? Or his failure to seduce May? Or because she had returned to Japan and he might never be alone with her again?

Or was he perhaps worried about what would happen if their little escapade were to be discovered? May was bound to be faced with some detailed questioning after her return. Would she be able to keep up the pretence of having spent two weeks with me, or would her stay in Paris be too much of an event to be concealed?

It was an interesting question, that last one. If Uncle Shin ever did find out that he had been deceived, he would undoubtedly be furious, but I guessed that he would keep the truth very quiet. Why should a silly girl's foolishness be allowed to spoil an arrangement which would be so useful to the family? I judged that he would have to forgive his niece, for the sake of the useful relationships which her marriage would bring him. But he was unlikely to feel charitable towards her escort – the man who had first of all suggested the trip to England and then had altered the plans in an underhand way. It seemed to me that Rufus had good cause to be worried. He might well at this moment be wondering whether it would be safe to return to Japan.

His immediate anxiety, though, was a more local and trifling one. He held me back behind the others for a moment as we all moved towards the drawing room.

"May I stay the night, Kit?" he asked abruptly. "I checked out of the hotel as soon as I heard . . ." He checked himself. May was not the only one who would have to watch her tongue.

"I'm sorry, Rufus, but I simply haven't got a spare room. I know this house looks enormous, but the whole of the top floor is green with mould."

"Tilda's room? Mayuko's room?"

By 'Mayuko' in this case he meant Hiromi, whose name he daren't use when her fellow-pupils might be listening.

"Mayuko" – I needed to follow his lead on names –

"slept in my mother's house, as you know, and Mum's got Bodger dumped on her now instead."

"Tilda's room, then?"

Why should I feel reluctant to agree? The room and its furniture belonged to me, and Tilda herself would never use it again. Once her father had arrived from Scotland to clear away her possessions it would become as impersonal as any other space. But until then, I simply didn't fancy the idea of allowing anyone – especially someone who had once been so intimate with her – the freedom to explore her books and notebooks and clothes.

"I really am sorry, Rufus," I said, thus putting two lies into one sentence, "but no one's to go in until the police tell me that they've finished with it."

"Oh, I see." His hangdog expression showed that he had got the message that I simply didn't want him to stay – since no one could claim that The Millstone is short of floor space or sofas.

"You're still angry with me, aren't you, Kit?" All the others had passed out of earshot by now. "For walking out on you."

"For heaven's sake, Rufus! That was years ago. Ancient history. And anyway, you're using the wrong words. You can walk out on a responsibility: a marriage or a steady relationship. But we never had that. You broke something off, that's all, and why not? We were both much too young to tie ourselves down."

For some reason he didn't seem to find that comforting. "I wish . . ." he said; and then tried to laugh. "I wish . . ." But this was clearly a different wish from the first one, because he reached out a hand to touch me. "I must say, all these bandages and bruises form a very effective chastity belt."

I might have suggested that I possessed even more formidable protective devices, such as the ability to say

No, but there was no need to be rude. Probably he wasn't so much interested in my body as needing to be assured that somebody in the world loved him. I felt sorry for him; but not sorry enough to become involved again.

Rufus was no longer the young man with whom I had once fallen in love. It wasn't only his body, but his whole personality which had lost the healthy self-confidence of youth. There was no humour in his eyes; no excitement when he spoke. Voice and body language combined to suggest that the whole world was against him. I could sympathise with the feeling; but I'd devoted a good deal of effort, at the time when Rufus and my hopes of a life abroad both disappeared at the same moment, to making sure that I would never feel sorry for myself. I had no intention now of being caught up in someone else's self-pity. Selfish? Yes. Sensible? Also yes.

Besides, I was still angry about the deception he had played on me and the deceit which he now expected of me in turn. It was that thought which made me change my mind. I needed to keep in touch with him while the search for Hiromi was in progress; and judging by the way he'd behaved in the past few days, that might not be easy.

"Well, all right," I said abruptly. "Come this way." I led him out of the house and across the courtyard to the coach-house. "You can sleep in Tilda's bed if you like. I don't suppose the police will be back before tomorrow morning. But for Christ's sake don't touch anything else in the room."

"OK. Thanks, Kit. I'm pretty bushed, so I'll hit the hay straight away. Thanks for everything. I really am sorry." He put a hand on my undamaged shoulder and I felt his grip tighten as he kissed me. It didn't mean a thing.

Back in the drawing room, I made for the coffee table. Holding a cup and saucer was still out, but I could raise a

142

cup to my lips with my right hand. Next duty was to call for silence and announce that Bodger was the evening's entertainment. Only then did I catch Sasha's eye and jerk my head to indicate that we could slip away.

I hoped that he wouldn't take the opportunity of a tête-à-tête to resume his earlier baby-making campaign, but reckoned that my plaster should provide sufficient defence.

"It's really good of you to come and cheer me up like this, Sasha," I said. "I owe you a million apologies for standing you up last night."

He had been an attentive pupil. Even in this ordinary conversation I could see him tucking away the phrase 'standing someone up'.

"It is easy to see that this was not your choice. The accident must have been very bad. How did it happen? Tell me please."

That was not a question to answer in detail, so I fudged it by moving sideways. "It wasn't so much the injuries as just being taken over. You know, put in an ambulance, dumped in a hospital. I couldn't suddenly sit up in the X-ray room and demand to use a telephone. And in any case, of course, once you'd left the office, I didn't know how to get in touch with you. How are you getting on at the office, Sasha? Do you enjoy the work?"

"I enjoy very much. I am working very hard so that when my university studies are over they will ask me to return to this office in London."

"That wasn't the idea, was it?" My understanding was that his training was being sponsored by a British firm so that he could act as its St Petersburg representative.

"Ideas may change. I wish to live in England, to become an Englishman."

My permanently raised eyebrows arched even higher, but I made no comment on this remark, and because we were walking side by side Sasha couldn't have noticed any signs of surprise. We were in the wood by now: it may have been the nearness of a bank of huge forest trees which prompted his next remark.

"I'm not like Jian-li, willing to be moved about like pawn on chessboard. When *he* goes back to China with his degree, he will be sent to manage a forest and he will not be allowed to choose the place, he said. He wishes to live in the east, near Beijing, but there is a committee which decides: you go here, you go there."

"Yes, I know." I had been told the system by Tilda in letters, and by another friend of mine, Nick, whose period of teaching had overlapped with hers but who had been back in England for the past year. "But his family will pull strings to get him the job he wants, I expect."

I could see that Sasha was tempted to query the phrase 'pull strings' but didn't want to interrupt the discussion.

"Only if he gets good degree, I think. Otherwise the family will feel disgrace. And he is stupid." Sasha's voice was contemptuous: the two young men had never liked each other. "I don't think he will understand what he is taught here."

"His English certainly isn't very good," I agreed. But it was not Jian-li who interested me at the moment. "Can we sit down for a bit, Sasha? I'm still feeling rather wobbly." One of the hornbeams had shed a huge branch during the second of the great gales and I had left the thickest part where it lay, to serve as a seat.

"Oh, poor Kit." He put his arm around my waist – to help me, I thought at first, but I soon recognised my mistake. So far from protecting me from amorous advances, my battered condition seemed to be acting as a general turn-on. I did my best to wriggle away; but it wasn't a very good best.

144

"No really, Sasha, please don't. This wasn't why . . . You're hurting me."

"Oh, I'm sorry." I couldn't stop him kissing me, but it did seem as though I had checked any further plans. "I don't want to hurt you. I love you so madly. What happened that night in your room was unfortunate. I thought that if you had baby you would be more pleased to marry me. But the baby doesn't matter. Just that you should marry me. Because I love you so much."

No, he didn't. Language is my skill, and I can always tell when words and emotions are out of sync. His motive for putting on an act was less easy to understand. Unless that was exactly what it was – a practise for his new enthusiasm, amateur dramatics.

"Please let go," was all I said. "You really are hurting me. There are bruises even where there aren't bandages."

His arms dropped to his sides. "But will you marry me?" he asked.

"Marry you! No, I won't, Sasha. I have no wish to marry anyone. I told you before. It's nothing to do with you personally." I had told him that as well, but it was worth repeating, knowing how easily his pride could be hurt. "I prefer being on my own, that's all."

"Well then, if you don't ever want to marry anyone else, you could marry me and I would go away and not be a nuisance to you."

So that was it. He was looking ahead to the time when his student visa would expire and he would have to go back to Russia. In order to stay here he would need British nationality, and the way to acquire that would be to take a British wife. For the sake of my own pride I was glad not to have been fooled.

"Don't ever do that again, Sasha," I said softly. "To me or to anyone else. To tell someone you love them when all

145

you really want is a new passport is unkind. And to bring a baby into the world just in the hope that its mother will feel forced to marry you is – well, it's dreadful." Not to mention being unrealistic. Sasha clearly hadn't cottoned on to the fact that not all women these days feel the need of a husband to go with the first-size baby clothes.

Just thinking about his campaign made me really angry, but for the sake of the questions which still needed to be asked, I had to prevent myself from walking off in a fury. But I needn't have worried that we were going to quarrel, for Sasha roared with laughter.

"Oh, clever Kit!" he exclaimed. "This is why I do truly love you, though you don't believe me: because you are clever and strong as well as beautiful." It seemed that the incident was over. He released me from his grip and allowed me to sit shakily down on the branch. "So you won't . . . ?"

"Definitely not. Please don't ask me again. Sasha, I wanted to ask you something. When you came to Oxford on the train on Wednesday, you said you recognised one of the other passengers. Who was it?"

His forehead furrowed with surprise at the unexpected question, but he did not hesitate before answering. "Jian-li was on that train."

"Oh yes, I remember you said so. But there was some-one else you mentioned. Someone who didn't recognise you because you were doing your Rasputin act."

"It's no one you would know. Someone I met a long time ago, when I was in England before."

"All the same, tell me the name, will you?"

He shrugged his shoulders. "Her name was Tilda. Miss Tilda Grace."

A torrent of relief flooded my body. I had been sure of it already. If Sasha had lied about it, I'd already decided

146

to abandon my questioning at once and leave it to the police to interrogate him.

Even this answer, of course, didn't prove anything, for there could be one of two different reasons for his ready admission. He might not know that Tilda was dead; and that would be good. Or he might know, but have no inkling of the fact that I had already established a connection between the two of them. How much more would he be prepared to tell me?

"How did you come to meet her, Sasha?"

"Why is this important? She was a foolish woman. For two, three years I have not seen her, and in the train we did not speak. All the time she read a book. She didn't know who I was, and I didn't wish to talk with her."

"I'll explain what it's all about in a minute. I've got a reason for being inquisitive." I already knew the answer to this question – and almost certainly to my next one as well; but once again it was important to discover whether Sasha felt that he needed to hold anything back.

He sighed, to show that he was humouring me under protest.

"Miss Tilda Grace was my teacher when I came the first time to England. In Bournemouth. Three years ago."

"And did you have an affair with her?"

"Why should you think so?"

"Because you're a sexy fellow and I'm sure she would have found you irresistible."

There was a very long pause before he made up his mind to come clean.

"Yes," he said at last. "I made baby with her."

"Did she tell you that?"

He shook his head. "It may be that she didn't know. There was not time. But I knew. In the moment of making, I knew."

"So what happened?"

147

"She went away!" he burst out. "There were more weeks of lessons to come, but she went away. Without telling me! As though nothing had happened. As though I was just one student, not more important to her than the others."

"You were angry with her?"

"Of course I was angry. She took my baby away."

"Your chance of marrying her, you mean. Your chance of persuading her to marry you, and getting British nationality."

For a moment his eyes remained dark with remembered rage. Then he laughed; his black moods never lasted for long.

"She was unkind to go like that. But she was no good."

"Do you still hate her? When you saw her in the train, were you angry again then?"

He shook his head. "No. It did not worry me. Three years is a long time. And I was coming to see you. I prefer to have you. Now you promised to tell me why you ask so many questions."

"I haven't quite finished." My next was one to which I didn't know the answer. "What did you do when you got off the train on Wednesday, Sasha?"

"I went to the court. To say that I had come."

That seemed to be the end of the answer, but I wanted more.

"Give me the details, Sasha. What time you arrived, how long you stayed, who saw you there."

"Have you become policeman?" he demanded. "How is this important?" But he could see that he wasn't going to get an answer. "Well, I went straightaway from the station to the court. Five, ten minutes walking. They told me the thieves should have come earlier but had not done so. But I should wait, in case they were only delayed.

148

Until half-past ten I waited. That was the time I was told to arrive. Jian-li came at exactly that time to join me. Then someone came to tell us about a letter saying that the thieves were already in Australia. She told us we could ask for our travel money and then go home. Jian-li was angry, shouting, but I didn't care. Although it took half an hour to get our money. And that is enough questions and answers."

Yes, it probably was. Sasha, wearing his Rasputin face, must have cut a memorable figure in the waiting area of the court. It sounded almost certain that one or other of the clerks would be able to give him an alibi until at least eleven o'clock, and by then Tilda was dead.

It was time for me to tell Sasha about the murder. His reaction was violent. He didn't seem to be at all affected by her death; only by my suspicions.

"This is why you ask so many questions? This is why you ask to meet me in London? You think I, I, Sasha kill a woman?"

"No. I wanted to make certain you hadn't. You did tell me that you were angry with her, remember."

"All finished. Long time ago. I don't talk about this any more." He was angry with me now – but showed no sign of wishing to strangle me. Instead, he stood up and began to stride through the wood towards the road, talking furiously to himself as he went. When he reached the drive he paused to look back, with good manners overcoming resentment. "Thank you for a very fine meal. Give my love to Maggie."

"No!" I exclaimed jokingly. To my amazement, he realised what I meant, and took a few steps back towards me.

"Why not?" In yet another shift of mood, he was smiling broadly. "A great lover for Maggie, and good meals for me for the rest of my life."

"Be off with you, Sasha." I too was grinning.

"Be off with you? Same as fuck off, yes?" He came right back to kiss me goodbye. We were friends again. I was glad, all the same, that he was not proposing to spend the night at The Millstone.

By the time I returned to the house, Bodger and his audience had adjourned to the library so that he could use the easel to illustrate his talk. I stood without interrupting while he finished a description of bridge-swinging. This seemed to consist of throwing oneself off one side of a bridge, attached to a rope, and swinging under the bridge to come up on the other side. To me that sounded dull, humdrum stuff. If there was any thrill to it at all, it sounded as though it would be jerky and soon over – quite unlike the orgasmic excitement of the double bungee-jump. Bodger may have been thinking along the same lines, because he brought the session to an end as soon as he caught sight of me.

"You ought to be in bed," he said, coming quietly to stand at my side. "I'm sure a day like this one isn't what the doctor would have recommended for someone discharging herself from hospital."

"You're quite right. I'm flaked out."

"That's not what I said. I said you ought to be in bed." He was steering me upstairs. It's my job to go round the house last thing at night, locking up, but I let it go. "I expect you need help with getting undressed." He had already started on the process before we reached my room.

"Bodger, this is no use. I shan't be any good to you." Tired and bruised, I knew that I should be too passive.

"That's not the point. I shall be good for you. And very, very gentle. Trust me. Like yesterday."

The memory of the previous day had another effect. I, just as much as Bodger, could play dangerous games.

There was no repetition of the bedroom scene with Sasha. I slipped away from common sense just as I had slipped from the bridge, and was rewarded with the same sensation of falling, falling, falling into bliss.

Chapter Twelve

Bodger spent the whole of the next day at The Millstone.
I was to rest, he told me firmly, and anyway the hour he
had spent discussing dangerous sports with my pupils had
given him a taste for teaching.

"They were telling me about these role play sessions
you organise for them," he said, setting a breakfast tray
down on the bed. "I thought we might do some job interviews this morning, with each of them in turn applying for
a job while all the others act as interviewers. And don't
say that you'd rather do it yourself, because I want a try.
Is there any back-up material I need to use?"

Role play ought only to be used as a preparation for
situations which are likely to arise, and only one of this
group was likely to be looking for a new job in the near
future, but I didn't feel disposed to argue. I often feel that
my pupils must get tired of the sound of my voice and
long for a change.

"Well, in my office there's a box of file cards, third
shelf down on the left," I told him. "You'll find one
section is labelled 'Interviews'. There are several groups
of six cards each. Those are for imaginary situations,
when you give one card to each of the girls, to tell
her who's she's going to be and what the facts are.
But they might enjoy it more if you make each in turn
describe some job she'd really like, and then you and
the interviewers can go into a huddle and settle on the

qualifications before you give her a grilling. Louise will probably want to be Queen of England! This is very kind of you, Bodger. But I shall come down for lunch, and take over again then."

He bent over to give me a smacking kiss. "It was a bit of all right last night, wasn't it?"

"A bit of all right," I agreed, and thought about that for a little while after he had gone. Then it was time to cope with breakfast. Black coffee and orange juice is usually enough for me, but scrambled egg flecked with anchovy proved too tempting to resist.

A few minutes of finger exercises suggested that my right hand was back to normal function again, although still black and swollen. I was able to call Mum and make sure that she too was recovering from her ordeal. Since she was equally concerned about me, we spent most of the time asking questions and not getting answers, but it was settled in the end that she would come up for lunch. Meanwhile I was to make an appointment with my GP to check that my abrupt departure from hospital had not caused irreparable harm.

"Incidentally," she said in a pretending-to-be-casual tone, "I seem to have lost another of my lodgers. Is there something about my spare bed that my best friends won't tell me?"

"He's here, teaching my class for me," I told her. "I needed Hiromi's passport and he very kindly brought it over." The next question, or the pregnant pause which might replace it, sent signals ahead while I was still speaking, so I closed the conversation with a cheerful, "See you at half-past twelve, then."

Bodger had brought up the complete delivery of daily newspapers with the breakfast tray. I turned over the pages. Most of the papers had reported the kidnap, but only two had printed the photographs and none of them

153

had made the point clearly that Hiromi's family would be in no position to pay a huge ransom. It was easy to reconstruct the police hand-out from the phrases common to each account, and I reckoned I could do better. After scribbling out a draft, I put a call through to the Bristol Evening News and dictated a story full of detail and local colour. On the strength of this I was put through to the news editor, who was quick to appreciate how he could take credit for Hiromi's release if his paper was able to convince the kidnappers that they would do themselves no good by holding her.

Sliding down under the sheet again, I prepared to make the most of an unexpected morning of leisure. There was no good reason why I shouldn't take a nap, but sleep didn't come easily. Instead, a kind of waking nightmare took over. I was a pillar, carved to look as though separate columns of stone had twisted round each other. I was a bindweed entwined with a honeysuckle. I was a rope, coiled round a capstan but entangled with a cable wound in the opposite direction. There was a message in every picture which made me jerk awake, forcing my eyes to stay open.

Why was I wasting time in bed when there were two puzzles to be solved? Where was Hiromi? Who killed Tilda? It was just because there were two problems that it seemed so hard to concentrate on one. Every time my thoughts moved off in one direction they were tugged back by the needs of the other. Hiromi's case was the more urgent, but I could hope that I had set the police on the right track to find her. Tilda's death was a different matter. There, I suspected, they were still on the wrong track.

Mort had been snubbed when he first took it for granted that Tilda's murderer and the rapist of Asian women were the same person, but everything he had told me since then suggested that his theory had been accepted. It was quite right that there should be a big hunt for the rapist; but not quite so right that this should divert questions away from other possible suspects. From that point of view it was Tilda – or her spirit – who needed my help. I hadn't got the resources to find Hiromi, but I had just as much information about Tilda as the police did, and rather more inclination to make use of it. And yet . . .

There I went again. As soon as I decided to investigate Tilda's murder, the thought of Hiromi rose up to worry me. Could the answer be that the two crimes were related and that somewhere in my subconscious mind I knew how?

If so, the relevant link was buried pretty deep. Superficially, of course, the connection was clear. Tilda's arrival in Oxford was an embarrassment to Hiromi and could have proved a disaster to Rufus and the real Mayuko. But Hiromi had dealt efficiently with the danger of a casual meeting. She could not be suspected of the murder and there was no reason to doubt that she had intended to return from Bristol with Mum and had genuinely been snatched against her will for money.

Rufus and May were a different matter. They had provided alibis for each other, with accounts of their morning in London together which meshed so perfectly that either they were true or else they had been carefully rehearsed. It was possible, in theory, that they had conspired together to prevent Tilda from revealing the imposture; but it didn't ring true to character. In apologising to me so unreservedly, May had impressed me as sincere. I judged her to be a basically sensible girl – sensible enough to realise when she had been foolish – and respectful and conventional into the bargain. A certain strength of character must have been required to keep Rufus at bay when she found herself almost at his mercy in a foreign country. It was inconceivable that she would knowingly have involved herself in a murder.

It did occur to me then, though, that there was another possibility. It was Rufus who had got her into a false position and she had to trust him not to expose her. Suppose he had pitched some kind of story, pretending that for her own sake she must claim they had spent the morning together, perhaps using the details of their activities on a different day. I remembered that although I had mentioned Tilda's name to her, in order to find out whether they were acquainted, I hadn't said anything about the murder. May might want to change her story when she knew that more was at stake than she had realised. It was something to be checked.

So what about Rufus, if his alibi should prove not to be watertight? He had admitted to a violent loss of temper once, but that experience might have been as frightening to him as to Tilda. It was possible, of course, that Tilda's death – whoever proved to have killed her – was the unintended result of a struggle which went too far. But my impression on meeting Rufus after such a long absence was that he had become passive and unambitious, allowing difficulties to overwhelm him rather than to stimulate him to action. I couldn't see him either pressing an argument to such lengths or planning and executing a cold-blooded murder.

It was time to remind myself that there were other people – not exactly suspects, but possible connections – who could be investigated without too much exertion. As soon as I reckoned that his lunch break would have started, I punched out on my bedside telephone the number of the Cambridge language school in which my friend Nick Roberts was working.

Nick, like Tilda and Rufus, had been on the first ELT certificate course that I took. The world of teachers of

English as a foreign language is a tight one. I'm an odd one out, staying in England, but most of the others follow the same pattern. For about ten years, until marriage and parenthood arrive to force consideration of such things as savings and homes and schools for children, they move round the world from one job to another, meeting each other briefly, hearing stories of a friend who has just left, giving opinions to a friend who is considering an application. "What a small world!" Mum tends to exclaim when I tell her about some unexpected renewal of contact; but that's not quite right. It's a network.

Nick had been a colleague of Tilda's in Beijing, his second year there overlapping with her first. After leaving China he had married and settled down to work in England. Once I'd got him to the staff-room telephone, I came quickly to the point of my call.

"Does the name Jian-li mean anything to you, Nick? A forestry graduate who was going on to do an English language course so that he could take a higher degree over here?"

There was a moment's silence for memory-searching before he answered.

"I know the one you mean. He did apply to us, but I don't know whether he got on the course. I marked his application test just before I left and advised Tilda not to accept him."

"Why?"

"I didn't reckon that he had a hope in hell of passing the course. Tilda's probably told you what goes on over there. You try to stop a weak student from enrolling; his family fires off its biggest guns and the chap is accepted. If the course is run by the Chinese themselves, the professor daren't let the weak pupil fail. But when the Brits are in charge, as we were on this particular course, the chap only gets the marks he deserves at the end of the year; so if he fails, the disgrace is total. He tells you that you're ruining his life, and it's probably true. It's much kinder not to let the student start in the first place. But of course he never really believes that anyone will dare to fail him."

"Did Tilda take your advice?"

"I don't think so. Her contract was due to end at the same time as the course, so nobody was really in any position to put pressure on her. She said it was time someone made it clear that not everyone would pass every exam, and that she'd warn Jian-li how hard he'd have to work if he wasn't to be one of the failures. A mistake in my opinion; but she was the one who would have to live with it. So presumably she did accept him. You obviously know something about him. Did he pass in the end?"

"Well, he's got a place at an agricultural college over here. And a grant. So it would seem that he did. But—"

"But you have your suspicions about whether he deserves them? Well, I could probably find out for you. Give me the name of the college he's going to. They'll have asked to see his certificate, so it will save time if I track down whoever signed it. He or she may be still out there."

"That would be marvellous of you, Nick." The prospect of having to cope with a Chinese telephone exchange had not been appealing. "Thanks so much. Sorry to be a nuisance."

"I'm glad of an excuse to chat with you." And for the next five minutes chatting was what we did, although it quickly became clear that his baby rated higher than Beijing as a topic of conversation.

Mum arrived punctually at half-past twelve to do a bit of mothering: helping me to dress, cutting up my lunch and driving me to the doctor's surgery. As he unbound the strapping and told me that what the shoulder really needed was not immobility but gentle movement, a progressive series of exercises, Dr Stanley didn't say in so many words that he thought the hospital had done everything wrong, but the implication was clear enough. However, he was politeness itself as he phoned to ask for my X-rays to be sent to the John Radcliffe, my local hospital.

"I'd like to have this plaster off as well," he told me as he put the phone down. "But I suppose we'd better wait for the X-rays to come through. In the meantime, you'll need a sling to take the weight for most of the time, but there's no need to feel nervous about doing without it when it suits you."

The freedom offered by the sling was only partial, but it felt marvellous. No longer constricted, I could breathe more freely: I felt a bigger, better person. It was easier to smile, and I was longing to get back to work. But there were still distractions. Tilda's father had arrived to clear her personal belongings out of the coach-house, under the supervision of a police sergeant whose duty was to note and possibly take possession of anything unusual. I watched for a little while after I'd spent some time expressing sympathy with Mr Grace. It was easy to tell that the police didn't really believe that anything in Tilda's own life had caused her death. She had just found herself in the wrong place at an unfortunate moment. The active murder enquiry was not going on at The Millstone, but down in the city.

It seemed surprising that Rufus hadn't come to say goodbye, but perhaps I'd been asleep when he left. The actual reason, it emerged later, was that he hadn't gone. I'd taken my class back into my own hands and was listening while each in turn made up a story from a strip of cartoon drawings when he came to sit at the back of the room.

Odd, what a feeling of awkwardness an observer can

induce in a teacher: it was almost as though I were a beginner, back on that first certificate course. Odd, as well, the lack of feeling which I had for Rufus. I regard myself as being good at maintaining friendships – and Rufus had been more than a friend. Well, perhaps that was the trouble. For the sake of my own peace of mind I'd had to seal off my love for him years before, and ordinary liking had disappeared with it. When I suggested that he should wait for me in the drawing room, it may have sounded like an invitation but was in fact an eviction order.

Half an hour later I found him sitting on one of the sofas, doing nothing. It seemed up to him to open the conversation, but I was the one who blinked first.

"I thought you'd left this morning." A stunningly original opening gambit.

"I wouldn't have gone without saying goodbye. And thanking you again. I wanted to wait – you've been so busy ever since I arrived. And so battered, poor Kit."

Once upon a time the sympathy in those moist brown eyes would have made me shiver with longing. Now I found myself reminded of a sloppy spaniel; and my thoughts moved straight on to wondering whether the Hearing Dogs organisation had found anything for Maggie yet. Rufus was putting on an act, and he wasn't a very good actor. Something of my impatience must have shown itself, because he came straight to the point.

"Kit, couldn't we try again?"

I could hardly pretend not to know what he meant, but that didn't prevent me from staring at him in disbelief. Since we don't live in a society which favours arranged marriages, there does need to be some flicker of physical attraction to start – or resume – a relationship. I felt nothing of the sort myself, and it was only a couple of weeks since Rufus had been longing to hop into bed with

May. While I struggled to think of some answer which wouldn't be downright rude, Rufus was pressing on.

"I've had time to realise, there's no future in allowing oneself to fall head over heels in love. It doesn't last. What survives is friendship. You and I—"

"Hold on, Rufus, before you start making claims. What you and I have had for the past eight years is silence, followed by deception. Hardly the best basis for friendship."

He leaned forward to touch my one available hand.

"I need you, Kit. You don't know what it's like to be adrift in the world, with no place to call home, no one to love and rely on."

So that was it. It seemed to me that I had good cause to feel annoyed. Sasha had wanted to marry me in order to get a British passport, and any moment now Rufus was going to make the same proposal in order to acquire a home. It was just as well, for the sake of my self-esteem, that there was Bodger, who was years away from contemplating marriage to anyone at all, but who certainly didn't regard me solely as being useful.

"I'm sorry, Rufus. I'm not in the market for providing emotional security for anyone at all. I've got enough responsibilities already – Maggie and the house – and I can only deal with them by feeling independent in every other way. Nothing personal." I'd said practically the same thing to Sasha as well, hadn't I? Well, at least I was being consistent.

"Is that really how you see your future? A spinster, growing older and older in a house which is collapsing around your head?"

"You're using out-of-date words. For 'spinster' try 'career woman'. And how I see my future is my business." My picture wasn't quite the same as his – that was for sure. I stood up, forcing him to do the same. To murmur platitudes about being good friends would not only be insincere, it would encourage his hopes. I said goodbye with a firmness which made it clear that the coach-house was no longer on offer.

That night I went to bed early. Bodger came too, but didn't stay. By half-past eleven he was back at Mum's house and I was asleep. At ten past twelve the telephone rang.

The voice on the other end was like nothing human. I'd often wondered who would buy the gadget which is advertised in mail order magazines by the inducement '*Amaze your friends: a choice of three ways to disguise your voice over the telephone!*' It appeared that they'd made at least one sale, for this was Mickey Mouse speaking. He squeaked only a single sentence.

"Your Jap girl will get into Oxford Railway Station at twenty-six minutes past midnight."

My first reaction was one of delight: feeding the newspaper with the story must have worked. Then I became anxious. There would be no buses running at this hour, and not much likelihood of a taxi waiting. I couldn't phone the police to report her release and ask them to pick her up, because it was necessary to get a story straight with her before she spoke to anyone else. I had to meet her myself, but to get from Headington to the station even in the dead of night would take ten minutes, and first I needed to dress. Scrambling into slip-on shoes and culottes, I threaded my plastered arm through the wide sleeves of a kimono jacket.

It would have been wise to find myself a chauffeur, but I didn't know whether any of my pupils drove at all, and certainly none of them was used to driving on the left. There wasn't time to wake them. If only I had allowed Rufus to stay on for another night! Luckily my Spacewagon is automatic and has power-assisted steering, so I should be able to do everything with my right hand, using the left one only to steady the wheel.

Keeping a grip on myself, to prevent too much haste from making me flustered, I started the car and made my way cautiously down the dark and silent drive before putting on speed. It was tempting to ignore the one-way system in the centre of Oxford, but any thoughts I might have entertained of taking a short cut through Queen Street were foiled by a large council vehicle parked in the middle of the road to spray water over hanging baskets. Forced to be law-abiding, I took the wide Oxpens circular route at the highest speed I could safely manage; but even so it was after half-past twelve when I arrived at the station.

There were no passengers to be seen. Perhaps the train was late as well. But no: when I eventually found someone to ask, I was told that it had arrived six or seven minutes earlier. Another question elicited the fact that two taxis had been waiting, and both had been taken.

Now I had something else to worry about. If Hiromi had been quick enough to leave the train and was now on her way by taxi to The Millstone, she would find the door locked and everyone asleep – I ought to hurry back. But suppose she had not been lucky with the taxi? Might she have started to walk in the direction of the bus stop which she had used before? I stood beside the car for a moment, undecided. If I were to drive off, the one-way system would prevent me from taking the route she was most likely to follow on foot. It was in that moment of indecision that I noticed a movement in the long-stay car-park.

There was nothing necessarily surprising about that. One of the passengers off the train might still be around, perhaps searching for a dropped car key. It might even – more likely – be a car thief. But I could see his shadow, and he was not staying near one car but moving away from the station in a furtive manner, taking care to avoid the security lights. And when I projected forward the direction he was taking, I was able to see the prey he was tracking. It was Hiromi.

Ducking low, I sprinted across the station approach road. I was still running when I heard a sound which chilled me – a gasping sound; the beginning of a scream, cut off before it could emerge.

The sound was nearer than I had expected. Hiromi, coming to a fence, must have been forced to turn back towards the station. As I approached, holding my breath lest even that that faint sound should alert the attacker, I was in time to see him bear her down to the ground, with one hand round her mouth and the other tearing at her clothes. Now she was lying face downwards, her body rigid: presumably she was too frightened to struggle. The man had his back to me. I had a few seconds in which to consider what to do, knowing that I would only have one chance.

I was in no condition to put into practice any of the unarmed combat moves which I had practised; and I carried nothing which could be used as a weapon. Except, of course, the plaster around my left arm.

That was enough. Using my right hand to lift the left arm, I twisted myself like a discus thrower before turning back with the whole weight of my body behind my plastered wrist. It hit him hard on the ear and temple: he collapsed, unconscious, on top of Hiromi.

I fell as well, unbalanced by my twisting. For a moment Hiromi must have been in danger of suffocation, for I was too dizzy with the pain in my arm to move. But she was able to wriggle free and crawl away.

"Hiromi! It's Kit here." I wasn't sure whether she'd

recognised me. "Run back to the station and find someone to call the police. Quick!"

How long would the man remain unconscious, I wondered as, staggering at first, she ran off. In any face-to-face fight I should certainly be the loser. It was tempting to play safe by sitting on his head, but I had no wish to become a murderer myself. Instead, and with some difficulty, I managed to pull one arm from beneath his body and turn it into an arm-lock. I put my good hand on his wrist, ready to pull if I felt him stir.

There was just enough light from the nearest security lamp to light up the scene. I had plenty of time to study the arm which I held in my power. It was freckled, and thick with gingery fair hairs. By the time a police car screamed into the car-park, I was laughing hysterically.

It seemed that I had caught the Oxford rapist.

Chapter Thirteen

Hiromi came running towards us between parked cars, showing the way to two uniformed policemen. She was dirty and bedraggled, her long black hair hanging unbrushed round her shoulders. The attacker was still unconscious, so I stood up and held her close while she shivered with strain and relief.

"Nothing more to worry about, Hiromi," I whispered. "You're all right now."

For a moment she was content to be comforted; but then looked up into my eyes, puzzled.

"Why do you call me Hiromi?"

It was a necessary reminder that she must be brought quickly up to date with everything that had happened since she disappeared. But there was no time to explain before one of the policemen straightened himself from his examination of the man lying on the ground and approached us to ask a question.

"Was the young lady, um . . . ?"

"No, thank God," I told him. "I got there in time. But there wasn't much doubt about what he had in mind. I hope I haven't killed him, have I?"

"No. Looks as if you packed quite a wallop, though. We'll need the young lady, and yourself, to come to the station and make a statement, but we won't keep you longer than necessary."

"Do you think this is the chap . . . ?"

He didn't answer the question in words, but the set of his lips and the glint in his eyes made clear enough what he hoped and believed.

There was a short discussion about transport. The wallop, as he called it, hadn't done my arm any good and I wasn't at all sure that I could drive safely. To attempt it under police observation would certainly have been unwise. We all waited until a second police car arrived. Then, while one of the policemen was driving my own car from the front of the station to pick us up, I had a necessary moment of privacy with Hiromi . . .

"I called you Hiromi because I know that's your name," I told her. "Now, listen very carefully. Your friend Mayuko, the real Mayuko, turned up after you disappeared, to tell me about this arrangement the two of you had made. She's gone back to Japan now. As soon as we've dealt with what has happened tonight, I must tell the Bristol police that you've turned up, because they have been looking for you. You are Hiromi now and you have been Hiromi all the time."

I paused, giving her time to nod.

"I expect the people who have been hiding you hoped for a high ransom – a lot of money – because they thought that you were Mayuko, but that was their mistake. Everything that you have done since you arrived and everything that has happened to you has happened to Hiromi. I have had two Japanese students, not one, in my class: Hiromi and Mayuko. Will you remember that? It's important for Mayuko's sake."

"But the others in the group will know . . ."

"Yes. I shall have to think of some story." How complicated it all was! It was fortunate that Hiromi was an intelligent girl: even after everything she had been through in the past few days she was quick to understand the situation.

167

The session in the police station looked set to be a long one. I was anxious – for reasons which I didn't want to explain – that Hiromi shouldn't be put to the strain and inconvenience of having to stay in England, or return, for the trial of her attacker. Fortunately the rape and near-murder of the girl from Singapore had provided semen specimens which could now be given a DNA check against tonight's prisoner.

"If they match, we've got him," I was told when I explained that Hiromi would not be in England much longer. "And I don't suppose your young lady tonight has much she could tell a court, if he came on her from behind. We'll get her to sign a statement. But your evidence will be more important, if you actually saw the attack take place. *You* aren't thinking of leaving the country, are you?"

Alas, no such luck. I signed my own statement and promised to defend it in court whenever necessary. That brought us to the moment when I had intended to reveal Hiromi's involvement, as victim again, in a second police enquiry. But I could see that she was completely flaked out and by now – at two o'clock in the morning – bed was definitely beckoning me as well.

We returned to The Millstone in convoy: a policewoman drove the Spacewagon, followed by another car to take her back. I don't go in for sleeping pills, but in the interests of later truthfulness I gave Hiromi a couple of aspirins for a genuine headache before she had a bath and put herself to bed in my room. Then it was time to do my duty as a citizen and put a call through to Bristol to report her return.

"She's had a sedative and gone to sleep," I told the detective who naturally enough wanted to speak to her immediately. I explained about the attempted rape. "She has described to me how she was driven to Reading

Station in a van and told she could catch a train to Oxford from there. I asked her where she was before that, and it sounds as though she was held first of all in a mobile home, like the one where you found my mother. Then she was whisked off in a hurry, in the middle of the night, and kept locked in the van after that."

Now that she was safe I was in no great hurry for her kidnappers to be found, since a quick arrest would make it necessary for her to be available as a witness, and too many secrets might be revealed. I felt sure that she would want to return to Japan as soon as possible, relieved to get away from a country in which abduction and rape appeared to be everyday occurrences. My mother, after all, had also been wrongfully imprisoned by the same villains, who had then done their best to murder me. Between us Mum and I could provide enough evidence if the police eventually caught up with the thug and his friends.

At last I was free to go upstairs. My bed is a double one, and somehow I'd expected Hiromi to be a neat, tight sleeper, leaving a share of the space for me. But as if to celebrate her release from imprisonment, she was sprawled diagonally, with her arms flung out. Sighing, I searched for my sleeping bag and went down to the drawing room sofa.

It was a bad night. My arm throbbed and, although the sofa was soft and long enough, it wasn't easy to change position in comfort. But insomnia did at least give me time to consider how best to ensure that Hiromi's fellow-pupils didn't spill the beans about May's escapade.

In the morning it was back to class as usual, except for Hiromi, who was instructed to rest in bed. I gave her a work-book in case she felt she wasn't getting her money's worth of teaching, but recommended sleep. She was still in bed, wearing a pair of my pyjamas, when Detective

169

Inspector Carey and his female sidekick arrived from Bristol for a second time. Reminding her that she was Hiromi until further notice, I left them to it.

By the time the detectives came downstairs again, the rest of my group had finished a preparation and vocabulary session and were playing out an airport scene which featured delayed planes and lost luggage. I was wielding the video camera in the role of a photographer awaiting the arrival of a pop star; but Louise, as the information girl who was getting tired of being asked by everyone how much longer the flight would be delayed, was delighted to take over from me. I led the Bristol contingent into another room.

"Have you got everything you want from Hiromi?" I asked them.

"Not yet. We shall need her to identify the place she was held, when we locate it. But she says she's not up to travelling just yet."

"I can believe that. To be attacked twice within a week was a bit rough. She was really done in last night."

"We'll be in touch, then. We shall want Lady Quilter for the same purpose, so perhaps they could drive over together."

"I'm sure that could be arranged." Liar. Not if I could help it, it wouldn't. I was clear in my own mind about what ought to happen next, and went up to see Hiromi as soon as her visitors had left.

She said exactly what I'd hoped and expected, after I'd made the necessary enquiries about her state of health.

"I have very much enjoyed studying with you. You are a very good teacher and I think my English is better now?"

"Yes, much better."

"But I would like to leave at once. To go home. Does this offend you?"

"Of course not. I quite understand. I'm sorry you've had such a bad time." For the sake of England's reputation, though, I couldn't refrain from pointing out that she had brought her troubles on herself by agreeing to impersonate Mayuko, to which she humbly agreed. "We'll need your ticket details to change the flight. You've got your passport back from Inspector Carey, haven't you. I'll drive you back to Heyford Close straight away. Now listen, Hiromi. When you are saying goodbye to the rest of the group, you are still Mayuko. Do you understand?" I had made sure that they hadn't seen any newspaper which carried a photograph of a second Japanese girl who claimed to be their fellow-student.

Hiromi understood the instruction, although not the reason for it, and I didn't give her much time to work it out.

"You've worked very hard in a short time, and you're much more fluent than when you arrived. If you want to prove to people what a good teacher I am, all you need do is hold your head up and speak out without hesitating. Will you do that?"

For a moment she dropped her eyes in the shy manner to which I had become accustomed, but then lifted her head and smiled.

"Yes, I will. I will be your advertisement."

"Good. Get dressed then, and we'll be off."

We left the others having lunch, and rang the airline from Mum's house. There was a flight that same evening: better and better. My intention, when I planned the airport role play earlier in the day, had been to drive the whole group to Heathrow and leave them busily tracking down specified bits of information while I saw Hiromi off. But Bodger overheard my telephone conversation.

"Would you like me to deliver her to Heathrow? I've

got to spend the next few days in London, and it's not much of a diversion."

"Would you really? It would mean staying with her to make sure there were no hitches."

"Another alternative career! English teacher yesterday; travel courier today. My CV becomes more interesting by the day. Yes, I will be responsible for getting her safely out of the country. No problem."

Before returning to The Millstone I was issued with a batch of Bodger's telephone numbers for the next fortnight, and in return wrote down the dates when I should be free of teaching duties. We were each happy about the prospect of keeping in touch. The break between courses couldn't come too soon for me this time. There was nothing wrong with my pupils, but my own extra-mural activities had proved distinctly over-exciting.

Leaving Hiromi to phone her family and pack her clothes, I returned to my duties, for it was time to give the group my full attention again.

During the next few days there were still distractions; but it was one advantage of teaching people to cope with real-life situations that real-life situations could be used as teaching aids. So when, for example, I was summoned to hospital to discuss my X-rays, my six attendants came too. Each was issued with a subject for a two-minute talk to be given later in the day and left to her own devices in the public areas of the John Radcliffe.

Two days after Hiromi's departure, Mort dropped in for one of his friendly chats.

"I hear you've been solving one of our cases for us, Kit my love. Catching the rapist. You'll find yourself being promoted to Detective Chief Inspector, I wouldn't be surprised. Except, of course, that there are plenty of other people down at the station fighting for the credit."

"It really was him, was it? I certainly thought so, but nobody seemed willing to say as much in words."

"They're willing enough now. He wrote a confession."

"Does that sort of thing count? I thought that nowadays you had to have your solicitor in attendance and a tape recorder going before you were allowed to incriminate yourself."

"That's when there's a judge to be satisfied. But this case isn't ever going to come to court."

"You don't mean that they've let him escape!"

"Only in a manner of speaking. He hanged himself in the police cell. Couldn't face the disgrace of it. A respectable sort of man he turned out to be – well, respectable on the face of it. Two children, pregnant wife, responsible job."

The news gave me a good deal to think about. I'd always understood that belts and ties and any other equipment suitable for suicide were taken away from prisoners. But it was none of my business if someone had been inefficient.

"You'll be needed for the coroner's court, Kit. But they've done this DNA business and there's no doubt that he's the one who jumped the Singapore girl as well as your young lady. So those two cases will be closed. The others will be left on file, but—"

"Does that mean that they're abandoning the investigation into my friend Tilda's murder?"

"Not much point in going on with it, is there, under the circumstances?"

There seemed plenty of point to me. "She wasn't raped. And it was in daylight, not at night. Did this chap confess to the murder?"

"It wasn't a specific kind of confession, as I heard about it. More rambling, like, about how he couldn't help it and how ashamed he was about the disgrace to his family. He

173

mentioned that there were eight girls. That's more than we knew about. I suppose some of them didn't like to talk about it."

"But did he confess to a death? If there was one attack which went so much further than the rest, he'd surely pick on that one to mention specially. A responsible job, you said he had. Now that you know who he is, has anyone checked where he was when Tilda was killed?"

"I'm sure they'll have thought of that, Kit my love." He was trying to soothe me, not liking to make it too obvious that a local beat bobby wasn't privy to the details of murder investigations.

"Can you find out for me? Just that one thing? Where he was at about quarter-past nine on that Wednesday morning?"

A bit put out by my insistence, he agreed to try, but I didn't give much for his chances. I could see how tempting it was to close a difficult case by loading it on to a suspect who could no longer be questioned. Of course that might be the true solution. But there again, it might not.

That evening I phoned my friend Nick again.

"Did you have any luck in checking Jian-li's qualifications?"

"I phoned the agricultural college where he's due to start in October. It was Tilda herself, apparently, who signed the certificate to say that he'd passed his English exam – and sadly, of course, we can't check that with her. So I've rung Beijing and asked one of the English staff there to get hold of the records and see if his name's on the list. I'm afraid it may not be too easy. We had to pass all our records over to the Chinese university authorities at the end of each year, so this will mean alerting them to the fact that there's been a query. If it turns out that there's been any hanky-panky, Jian-li could find himself in trouble."

That didn't worry me too much. I could only get him into trouble if trouble was what he deserved. I added a note to the list of things to be done next day. It would be interesting to learn from the college registrar whether Tilda's signature was on an original certificate or a photocopy.

Chapter Fourteen

The agricultural college which had accepted Jian-li for a forestry course was up in the north, near the Scottish border. It was vacation time, so almost all the staff were on holiday and I had to do my best over the telephone with a secretary who was not prepared to take responsibility for anything at all. I did my best to give the impression that I was the Principal of something to do with Oxford University, but only after a good deal of pressing did she agree to open Jian-li's file and answer my question.

"It does seem to be a photocopy, the English language certificate. He's sent the original document for his forestry degree. I suppose he thought that was the only important one."

"And is it?"

"Well, no, the students are told that all supporting documents which are specifically required must be the originals. And must bear the name and address of the issuing authority, so that we can check. You'd be surprised. People come up with diplomas from universities which don't exist. Or else exist only as a small office somewhere just for the purpose of selling certificates. There's one in Arizona . . ."

I let her babble on, without bothering to listen too carefully, knowing how dull it could be to be stuck alone in an office all day with everyone else on holiday. But in fact nothing she was saying surprised me at all. My years of teaching had taught me how much could be at stake for an ambitious young man or woman who needed a recognised western degree.

"Do you think you could send me a photocopy of your photocopy?" I asked when at last she had exhausted the subject of non-existent universities.

"Oh no! I'm sorry, Miss Quilter, but the students' files are completely confidential."

"Well, perhaps you could tell me when the registrar will be back in the office."

"September the first. It's Mr Graham."

"And by that time would you expect to have received Jian-li's original certificate? That's to say, has he been asked to send for it, or have you waived your requirement?"

"I wouldn't know about that sort of thing. I'm sure his acceptance would have been conditional on all the rules being kept."

I could recognise a fudge when I heard one. They hadn't intended to bother, because in a sense it didn't matter to them. The Chinese government would be paying Jian-li's fees, and if he couldn't understand what was going on when he turned up for classes, hard cheese. It was at the Chinese end that language competency would be regarded as important. But thanks to Nick's work on my behalf, my enquiry about that certificate was probably the second one she'd had to field within two days. Now that I'd signalled my intention of putting the same questions to Mr Graham, the secretary – if she had any initiative at all – ought to make sure that he would be in a position to give the right answers. It would be surprising if Jian-li, somewhere in the Kielder Forest, didn't receive a note within the next few days, reminding him that the certificate was needed.

The delay didn't matter. Nothing could bring Tilda

back to life again, and Jian-li would be in the country for the next twelve months. I abandoned that line of enquiry for the moment and turned my thoughts in a different direction, considering the possibility that Mayuko might have been lying when she provided Rufus with an alibi. That was something else to be checked. And at some point – trading on my credit as the rapist-catcher – I ought to sweet-talk Mort into asking some more questions about the inquiry into Tilda's death. Had she been robbed, for example? Where had she spent the last night of her life? Who was it who had expected to lunch with her, and had he made any enquiries when she didn't turn up? Once my course was over, I could devote myself full-time to solving the mystery; but there was no hurry.

For the last week of the course I gave even more attention than usual to my pupils, to make up for the disturbed period in the middle. The days passed quickly: I was almost taken by surprise by the end of the four-week period.

By then my shoulder and other damaged parts had almost healed and no longer needed plaster or bandages. We always have a party on the last night of each course: an occasion to remember, I hope. This was a perfect summer evening at the end of a perfect summer day. The lilies had decided to forgive me for allowing a helicopter to attack them and were pumping out scent until the air was almost too perfumed to breathe. We all wore our best frocks as we assembled on the terrace. I'm only rarely to be seen in a skirt, but it's good to feel young and frilly once in a while.

Maggie does marvels on these occasions, producing plates of titbits to get the occasion going, with an elegant buffet waiting for later in the evening. She must work out the decoration of all the dishes entirely from cook-book illustrations, because I doubt whether she's ever been a guest at a smart party in her life. My contribution to the catering is in the drinks department. In winter I brew a wicked mulled wine, but for an August party my speciality is a fruity and fortified wine cup which kicks enough of a punch with the first sip to induce the party spirit and is gently diluted into a less lethal mixture as the evening wears on.

I started by taking photographs, individually and as a group. This was the moment – while they were all excitedly chattering about their clothes and the wine cup – when I was able casually to raise the subject of their Japanese fellow-student. There should have been two, I told them: Mayuko and Hiromi. But one of them had messed up her arrangements and the other had had to return early for family reasons: no need to specify which was which. So neither of them had really become part of the group, had she? And what a good group it had been. And I hoped they – these six – would keep in touch with each other because international understanding was so important and whatever might happen to them in the future they would all have this four-week period in common as part of their lives, a shared experience in England. Blah, blah, blah.

My intention was to turn Hiromi aka Mayuko into a non-person, someone who had hardly been a member of the group at all. It would be easy to tell later on whether I had succeeded, when they all started exchanging addresses. With a bit of luck no one would pipe up with, "What a pity about Mayuko!"

Certainly no time was allowed for thinking now. Their education was not yet complete, I announced, and before they went near the buffet they must work up an appetite by learning a Scottish dance. I had the music on tape and brought out the cassette player. Even plugged in to the cable extension reel it didn't quite reach the terrace,

179

but one of the advantages of living in a house like The Millstone is that there are no close neighbours. No one ever complains when I turn up the volume, because there's no one within earshot.

So for the next half-hour or so there was a good deal of shouting on my part and giggling and bouncing about by everyone else while the music boomed on despite the confusion. It was after we had all flung ourselves down on to the grass, panting and laughing, that I noticed Rufus, standing under the trees at the far end of the lawn.

How long had he been there, I wondered; and what did he want? After his night in the coach-house he had said goodbye, and I hadn't expected to see him again. He didn't make any movement towards me when our eyes met, but his body language spoke clearly enough. He was hoping to join the party.

Once upon a time I would have waved a cheerful hand. All comers welcome. Make yourself at home. But not now; not Rufus. As I deliberately turned away and suggested one more perfect run through the dance, now that they all knew the steps, there was a flicker of shame in my heart. But I wasn't an insouciant student any longer. I'd gone to a lot of trouble to form a bond between these six women and I didn't want it spoilt. Seven females can have a good party together. Add one male to the recipe and the party is in danger of becoming a competition. My movement made it clear – first that I'd seen him, and second, that I hadn't seen him. Mean, I know.

The music ended and it was time to eat. I gave Maggie the signal to whip off the sheet of mosquito netting with which she had covered one of three long tables and then led the way round to the tennis court on which the buffet was laid out. At the sight of its centrepiece, a fine salmon elaborately decorated with shrimps and samphire and cucumber and mayonnaise, there was a

180

spontaneous outburst of clapping. Maggie, ready to serve, stood behind the table, beaming with pride and happiness. I poured wine and reflected, as everyone loaded plates with a variety of salads, that there was enough on the table to feed twenty and yet I was begrudging Rufus a share. Mean, Kit; very mean.

At least an hour passed before everyone had finished their successive helpings of the three different puddings and we all carried our coffee cups back to the main terrace. It was time for party games, I announced, wondering whether there's anyone else in England besides me who still enjoys this old-fashioned activity. Adults at parties do nothing but drink; and children's parties nowadays tend to be video shows or discos. But I still trot out the games I used to enjoy twenty years ago, when I was nine – and they're just the sort to make foreign students feel good about being able to cope. Flower, fruit, animal, tree, eight other categories and your letter this time is . . . P. Or 'I'm not Napoleon'. Or 'In The Manner Of The Word'. That sort of thing. Even charades and Drawing Clumps work, because all the guessing is in words.

Next morning, as we all recognised, there would be a general rush for the express coaches to Heathrow and Gatwick, for only Radhika was staying on in Oxford. So in the course of the evening each of my pupils found an opportunity to say their thank-yous. By the time the last of them went up to bed I was feeling pretty smug. I'd be no good at controlling inner-city adolescents who equate school with prison, but it's a satisfying job helping highly motivated adults who appreciate intensive teaching and who can recognise their own improvement at the end of even such a short course. As I wandered into the kitchen to help Maggie with any remaining clearing-up I was not as near to being drunk as on the last evening with

181

Sasha and his friends; but I was certainly – well, shall we say, happy?

Rufus was in the kitchen, finishing up a raspberry mousse, with an empty plate nearby to show that he had already done his duty by the salmon. For a moment I was prepared to be annoyed with Maggie – but that wouldn't be fair. She knew that I had let him spend a night in the coach-house, so she must have taken it for granted that he was a friend. And how could I begrudge her the chance to be generous with the spread she had so generously provided? What she wanted from me was a big thank you, and the assurance that she had made a magnificent contribution to the evening's success; so that was what I gave her.

Perhaps Rufus had been acting as kitchen maid; there was nothing left for me to do except to unload the dishwasher. By the time I'd finished that he was standing up, waiting to have my attention.

"Could we have a word, Kit?"

"OK. Drawing room." I lingered to thank Maggie once more before joining him there. My guess was that he was about to say goodbye. Had it not been for the death of Mayuko's grandfather, the next day would have seen her departure from England under the pretence of having finished the course; and presumably Rufus was booked by the same flight. But that guess was wrong.

"May has blabbed," he blurted out as soon as I joined him.

"You amaze me! Taking her to Paris, when that could never have been on my timetable, was a crazy idea."

"That was all I could offer to persuade her to abandon you. But yes, I suppose it was too much to hope that she'd be able to resist mentioning that part of her visit. Not that she meant to, I gather. She bought a lot of clothes. The label on one of the dresses gave it all away, and she confessed."

As anyone might have anticipated, I thought to myself, but presumably Rufus had some reason nearer home for wanting to tell me this.

"I had a letter today from her uncle, with translation appended. It will not be appropriate for me to return to Japan. The language school I was working for has been persuaded to terminate my employment. Or, more accurately, not to renew my contract. He enclosed a sterling banker's draft. Compensation, he said. Hush money, really."

"How much hush?"

"Ten thousand pounds."

I whistled in appreciation without feeling the need to be sympathetic about his dismissal. The teaching of English to foreigners is one of the very few fields of employment in which it's almost always possible to find some sort of job, if you're not fussy about places like Ankara and Jakarta. Presumably Rufus wouldn't much have enjoyed returning to Japan in any case, now that he had lost Mayuko.

"You could pretty well set up a school of your own somewhere with that, couldn't you?"

"No, it wouldn't be enough." I could tell from the tone of his voice how much the idea would have appealed to him, though. "I wondered, Kit . . . This house of yours must cost a fortune to keep up."

There was no point in turning down whatever he had in mind before hearing what it was, but my eyes narrowed discouragingly as I waited.

"I wondered if I could come into partnership with you. Business partnership. I realise that ten thousand wouldn't anywhere near match the value of your house, but as cash in hand it could be useful, couldn't it?"

183

"What exactly are you suggesting? What would you expect for your ten thousand?"

"It would be marvellous if I could live in the coach-house. I haven't got a home in England. Or anywhere in the world, really. But I'd want to be a working partner. Helping you with the teaching. We could take twice the number if there were two of us. With a bit of cash to do repairs, you could bring all those rooms at the top of the house into use."

What did he mean by 'partner', I wondered. If he were to accept only the wage of an assistant teacher, plus his lodging, the capital sum would be irrelevant. If he was looking at the money as an investment entitling him to a share of any profits, then there were circumstances in which I could find myself a heavy loser. It wasn't nearly enough.

Only a week or so earlier, seeing him adrift in the world, with no roots, no ties, I had felt sorry for him; and I was sorry again now, forcing myself to consider the proposition seriously. My emotions told me at once that any arrangement of this kind would be a hideous mistake. I would simply land up with a third millstone, to add to Maggie and the house, hanging round my neck. But he was suggesting a business arrangement and it seemed only fair to look at it in a businesslike way.

To pretend to, at least; but even as I started to talk through the possibilities I could tell that the decision had already been made. So, no doubt, could Rufus.

"Doubling the numbers would put the whole operation on a different scale," I said slowly. "Maggie would have to have help with the catering." That would be a complication to start with, because Maggie didn't get and didn't want a wage for all her work. It was understood by both of us that she was a member of the household and could take whatever money she needed

184

from the housekeeping. Almost invariably she received a present from each group as a course came to its end, and whenever I was consulted on the subject I indicated that money would be more welcome than any gift-wrapped parcel. There was an insurance policy, whose premiums I paid myself, which ensured that if she survived me she would not be left penniless. Her position, in a financial sense, was that of a man's dependent wife – a wife of the old-fashioned kind – but she trusted me and was happy with it. To introduce a paid assistant into the kitchen would risk upsetting the balance. "And we'd need more cleaning help as well."

"All that could easily be arranged. I would be self-financing."

I was silent for a few moments longer, and then came out with a statement which was true in its own right, without taking into account any uneasiness I might feel about working closely with Rufus.

"I tell you what worries me, Rufus. The way I work at present, having just six people to stay here, I can feel – and so can they – that they're house guests. They have the run of the whole place, there are hardly any rules and even in a short time I can form some kind of a relationship with each of them. Double the numbers, and suddenly I'd find myself running a hotel and a school. That's not what I want."

"It's the way to become profitable. To build on your success. You don't want to plod on in exactly the same way for the rest of your life, surely?"

"You said this to me once before, but what's so wrong about it? Most people who are lucky enough to have jobs are stuck in them for life. I'm far more fortunate than most because I enjoy my job so much and it's never monotonous."

"You used to be ambitious once, Kit." His voice

185

was soft, attempting a return to the intimacy we had once shared.

I shook my head. "No. I suffered from wanderlust once, just as you did. That's not at all the same as being ambitious. Almost the opposite, in fact."

"If you had a partner, you could take off for a year from time to time."

That was certainly true, and for a moment it made me pause. A leakproof roof and a year's sabbatical combined to provide a powerful bribe. But in the end I shook my head for a second time.

"I'm sorry, Rufus. Thank you very much for the offer, but I can't accept it. I like being on my own. I want to run my own show."

"Well, couldn't I—"

"No." Whatever the suggestion, the answer was going to be No. Defeated, he stood up to leave. I realised that I was never likely to see him again and there was a moment in which the realisation hurt, just as Tilda's death had hurt. If he had stepped forward to kiss me then, I wouldn't have slapped his face; but he didn't.

"Rufus!"

"Yes?"

Was it foolish of me to be worried for his safety? The arrival of a cheque made it clear enough that Uncle Shin was the sort of man to believe that anything could be bought with money, so why should he contemplate trying to silence Rufus by any other means? No, of course there was nothing to fear.

"Take care, that's all. There are villains about."

He didn't smile. He didn't say goodbye. He just left.

As for me, I could have shrugged my shoulders. I could have felt regret. What in fact I chose to do, although it was long after midnight, was to write an airmail letter to Mayuko.

I hadn't liked to write earlier, in case she might have difficulty in keeping her correspondence private. But if the secret of her escapade was already known to her uncle, no further harm could be done.

'Do you remember that I wanted to know how you had spent your first Wednesday morning in London?' I asked; and repeated the details she had given me about Harrods and sightseeing. 'You may have thought at the time that the question was not important. But something happened on that morning which makes it very important for me to know whether what you told me was true. Did Mr Fergie perhaps make up a story for you to tell? Or did he suggest that what really happened on a different morning should be described as if it happened on the Wednesday? I promise that nothing you tell me will make any trouble for you.'

My assurance was genuine enough, for she had made no statement to the police. I was conscious, though, that for fear of frightening her into silence I had deliberately refrained from making any mention of murder – especially since the murder victim was someone she knew.

It was tempting to add a new English phrase for her to learn: 'You owe me one'. But it wouldn't be necessary; her own sense of honour would say it for me. After I had finished writing, the letter lay for a while unsealed in front of me. I thought I wanted to find out who had killed Tilda, but would I really want to know if the answer proved to be Rufus?

Chapter Fifteen

After the flurry of departures came peace at last. By noon the next morning Radhika had been collected by her sponsor and I had driven the other five and their luggage to the lay-by opposite the Park-and-Ride. Here they could catch express coaches to the airports or to London, to join the Eurostar train. I waited in the Spacewagon for half an hour, prepared if necessary to drive anyone who failed to get a seat; but my Good Samaritan act was not required. As Louise, the last to go, waved goodbye, all my responsibilities slipped away and I could feel my exhausted mind and body stretching themselves to fill the space. Freedom!

By the time I returned to The Millstone, the big monthly clean-up was in progress. Dorothy, our regular cleaner, brings along her sister for the day to help turn mattresses and move furniture for carpet-sweeping. Together they scrub and polish and generally return the guest bedrooms to luxury hotel standard. Maggie also has one last morning of hard work in the domestic quarters: cleaning silver in the butler's pantry (yes, The Millstone is that kind of house), emptying vases in the flower pantry, and making sure that the kitchen itself, always immaculately clean, could if necessary, double as an operating theatre. After that she, like me, is on holiday. For the week after the end of each course, once the buffet left-overs are finished, we both live on scrambled eggs or beans on toast.

On this occasion, though, it seemed that her mind was not on her work. She was watching for my return and dashed out to greet me with a piece of paper in her hand. It was a telephone message, written down by Dorothy, which had made her as excited as a child.

'Phone call. Hearing Dogs for Deaf. Mary Butler will call at 2pm with possible dog.'

I signed my pleasure at the news, but then wrote a cautionary message on the pad hanging from Maggie's belt. I'd been warned that a first visit would be only exploratory: there would be no question of handing over the dog on the spot. Before going further, the animal and the human must find out whether they liked each other – whether the chemistry was right. If it was, the trainer would spend time studying the geography of the house and Maggie's particular needs. Then she would take the dog away to teach it what precisely to do, before returning for a further training session with Maggie herself. I didn't want Maggie to be disappointed by the delay; but her eyes were still bright with pleasure as she nodded vigorously to show her understanding.

When the time came, I was the one who was disappointed. I don't much like dogs which are small. There's no good reason for this – I just don't. They seem to be more restless than their larger relations, and to bark more, often with the sort of yapping which drills into the head. So my heart didn't exactly leap up when I saw Mrs Butler get out of her car carrying a Pekinese. It wore a yellow ribbon to keep its hair out of its eyes and its name was Coco. Neither of these facts did much to endear it to me. I had to remind myself that this was to be Maggie's dog, not mine, and that presumably it would be trained to realise that there was no point in barking, since its owner would only respond to touch.

Maggie loved him at sight. She bent down and put out a

189

hand, just as she used to do every morning with Griselda, and the peke promptly put a paw on her palm. I was the one he wanted to play with, though. As we showed Mrs Butler round all the parts of the house which Maggie frequented, he sniffed around my ankles. And when we all sat down in the drawing room he immediately jumped on to my lap, circling two or three times like a cat before settling down for a nap.

"Say 'No' and push him off firmly, will you?" asked Mrs Butler. He was not to be allowed to think even for a moment that I was his charge. That suited me: I stood up and suggested that it would be best if I left the three of them alone. I would go for a stroll in the wood and return in an hour.

I love walking in the wood. It's not a very large one; a considerable amount of zig-zagging is necessary to make a walk last for an hour. But it's very old. Headington was a royal manor in Saxon days, so some of these trees, by natural regeneration, must be directly descended from those which stood here when kings and courtiers hunted in the forest even before the Normans arrived. Others, which are not indigenous, were introduced by my own family, but still a long time ago.

The oldness of the trees gives me enormous pleasure. Some of them are huge – absolutely huge. I like to think of my grandfather playing there as a boy; building the tree house which survived to enliven my own childhood visits. I like to think of my grandmother as a young bride, watching her gardeners plant hundreds of snowdrops and daffodils and bluebells. They have increased to thousands now, and still paint the ground with colour during their seasons. I like to think of some earlier ancestor planting the trees – and perhaps sparing a moment to wonder about the descendants who would walk in them one day. I had just plunged into the wood, and was reflecting on those ancestors, when Jian-li stepped out from behind a gigantic chestnut.

The unexpectedness of his appearance made me gasp aloud.

"You startled me!"

"I am very sorry."

"What are you doing here, Jian-li?"

"There is something to show you," he said. "I am walking up to the house to see you, when I notice this tree. Hornbeam. Very sick." He was still, I observed, confining himself to the present tense in spite of all my efforts. But at least he had successfully learned the English names of trees.

Waving a hand to indicate direction, he led the way further into the wood and for a few steps I followed him without thinking. Then I stopped dead, asking myself how he had come to notice a hornbeam which could not be seen from the drive. That was when I remembered Tilda, and suddenly the friendly wood turned sinister.

My vague and unprovable suspicions of Rufus ought not to have made me forget that Jian-li was also high on the list of suspects. He had travelled on the same train to Oxford as Tilda, and since – according to Sasha – he had seen the back of Sasha's head, then he must have seen Tilda's face. If he had indeed created a false photocopy of his certificate – either by pasting Tilda's signature from some other document on to a blank form or, more probably, covering the name on a friend's certificate with his own – he might have been thrown into a panic by seeing her in England. I could have assured him that her mind at that moment would have been only on her forthcoming interview; but Jian-li was quite enough of an egoist to have suspected that she was tracking him down in order to betray him.

All those thoughts were vague and inconclusive, and

191

the only thing which had persuaded me to give them any weight at all was Sasha's information about how vital it had been for Jian-li to pass what anyone here might think to be an unimportant exam. It was not just the disgrace of failure, but the prospect of being banished from Beijing to some remote and uncivilised area for the rest of his life.

It didn't take long for all this to flash through my mind; but what brought me to a halt was the realisation that he could have learned of my meddling in his affairs. Within the past few days he had probably received a request to produce the original of his certificate; and it was all too easy to imagine him phoning to make some excuse and being told by that stupid secretary about my enquiry.

I didn't really believe that I was in any danger. People don't get killed in their own woods – at least, not when I am the people concerned. I ought perhaps to have remembered that people don't often get thrown off bridges, either – and that on this occasion there was no Bodger at hand to come to the rescue. So I wouldn't say that I was frightened at that moment; but just wary enough to turn away.

"I'm sorry, Jian-li, but I haven't time now." I tried to keep my voice light and natural. "I've got an appointment with someone at the house."

This, unfortunately, was not true. Although I had a dinner date with Bodger, to celebrate my first free evening, I didn't expect him to pick me up before six. Having produced the lie, I added a useful embellishment.

"If I keep him waiting, he'll come to look for me, and I don't want to put him to that trouble. Why don't you come up to the house with me and say hello to Maggie? I'll come and look at the hornbeam with you when you're leaving."

He didn't believe me. "No. Now." His hand gripped my arm tightly. "I show you. The bark is peeling and parasites are eating, eating. Soon the tree is dying, and then the branches fall, very dangerous." He still pronounced 'very' as 'velly', although I had spent far longer with the skull and the tongue, trying to get that right, than May had needed to perfect her 'please'.

"Let go, Jian-li. You're hurting me." The John Radcliffe hospital had replaced my plaster with a firm bandage, and on a second visit had told me that I was healing nicely; but I was still pretty tender. What was even more to the point – since Jian-li showed no sign of loosening his grip, and by now was almost dragging me along – was that I had no hope of fighting him off. He was a strong young man, as I remembered from his fight with Sasha.

So I didn't struggle, but did my best to conceal my alarm and pretend that I hadn't noticed anything untoward. Through his grip I could feel the simmering of Jian-li's anger at my interference, but perhaps all he needed was to express it and then have done. I might have made myself believe that if it hadn't been for Tilda.

As we approached the hornbeam, I noticed at once that something was different. Only a few days earlier I had sat side by side with Sasha on one of its fallen branches. There was some reassurance to be found in the fact that Jian-li was not inventing the diseased state of the tree. I knew already that it was unsafe in a high wind. What had changed was that the branch was no longer lying along the ground, but had been propped up against the trunk. It was large and unwieldy. If Jian-li had lifted it alone, he was even stronger than I had realised.

"Yes. Yes, I see what you mean." It was a last effort to appear unconcerned. "I'll get a tree surgeon to come and look at it. Thank you very much for drawing it to my attention. And now—"

Once again I tried to free my arm, but instead found it twisted behind my back in an arm lock so painful that I

193

cried out. Almost as a reflex action I kicked up towards his groin, but he saw my foot coming. Releasing my arm and grabbing the ankle instead he sent me crashing to the ground. He followed me down, something my body with his own. His weight forced all the air out of my lungs. I struggled first of all to breathe. Only then could I attempt to free myself. But before I had time to move I felt my wrists being pressed close together and entwined with wire.

He had had his snare ready. As I struggled unsuccessfully to free myself I could see that the other end of the wire was already fastened round the trunk of the tree, ensuring that I could not move more than a yard away. It was a thin cheese wire, sharp enough to draw blood as I tried to move my wrists apart, but strong enough to hold me. I could feel the taste of panic in my mouth.

"Why do you do this?" he demanded. "I am told there is no place for me at college in England unless a new paper comes to say that I understand English well. You know that I understand. Why do you make mischief? Why?"

"I don't know what you're talking about." Should I scream, I wondered. But I had walked too far from the house. Maggie would not hear, of course, and any sound would be too faint for Mrs Butler to recognise as a cry for help.

"You ruin my life. I am young man with good degree, but now there is nothing for me. Who will marry a man who is sent to Sin-Kiang?"

"If you hurt me, you'll find that there are worse places than Sin-Kiang." Wherever that might be. "Like the inside of a British prison for the rest of your life."

"No one knows I am here. You will have an accident, very unfortunate. You should not sit under a dangerous tree."

He was standing over me, legs apart, revelling in his

194

power. Was he going to stamp on my head? Instinctively I turned my face to one side. It was humiliating as well as frightening to be lying on the ground, unable to lift my shoulders more than a few inches. As he gestured with his head towards the branch of the tree which he had propped against the trunk, I could see all too clearly what he had in mind. Yes, a branch was indeed going to fall, and no doubt he would finish the job off himself if necessary before removing the wire.

"The police know who killed Tilda," I said. "They'll know who to look for if anything happens to me."

"Also an accident," he claimed. I didn't believe him; but that one phrase was enough to tell me that he had indeed been responsible for her death. It suddenly seemed even more important than before that I should survive to make the truth known.

He began to move away, towards the propped-up branch. While his eyes were off me, I used my feet to push myself nearer to the tree. Now my head and shoulders concealed my hands from view. They had been fastened in front of me and not behind my back.

The wire which stretched from my wrists to encircle the tree was only a single strand. I gripped it in two places, holding it tightly immovable with one hand and twisting it as fast as I could with the other. I could feel the blood beginning to gush as the thin wire cut into my fingers and thumbs, but there was no pain. That – and the satisfaction of knowing that I was not simply lying like a dummy, waiting for whatever might be going to happen – helped me to keep my voice calm as I tried to keep him talking. Every moment that passed was a moment in which a miracle might occur.

"How did it happen?" I asked.

There was a sense in which I didn't want to hear the answer. The truth could prove dangerous knowledge. If

195

he was prepared to reply, he would already have decided not to give me any chance to pass on what I was told. But the need to keep the seconds ticking by was stronger.

For once his limited grasp of English tenses was not restrictive, but instead added drama to his story. He made no mention of recognising her on the train, so that guess of mine must have been wrong. But as he spoke I could see as vividly as though I had been there the encounter with Tilda at Oxford station as she turned away from the locker in which she had deposited her suitcase. Her teasing suggestion that Jian-li had presumably come to England to look for a better teacher, since she had not done him well enough herself; and her claim – when he mentioned my name – to be a friend of mine.

Listening helplessly, I was overwhelmed by a great sadness on Tilda's behalf. If only she had not turned at that precise moment. If only, once the meeting had taken place, she had not made it clear that she was on her way to The Millstone and looking forward to a chat with me. It was easy to see how quickly a self-centred young man would assume that – because he was known to both of us – we should immediately compare notes on him.

Jian-li was still talking, in an angry, high-pitched voice. I could imagine Tilda's friendly smile when he offered to carry her cabin bag to the bus stop in the Cornmarket, and the slight frown which would have puckered her forehead when she realised that, talking vigorously, he had turned her along the path on the wrong side of the canal: the path which led only to wasteland. He was trying to persuade her to agree to something – but at that point, my attention was distracted. A car had turned off the road and into The Millstone's drive.

It was a hot day. The windows – and perhaps even the roof – of the car would be open. It was not going to come very close to where I was trapped, but I tracked it with my ears until it reached the nearest point. At that moment I screamed.

Moving faster than I would have expected, Jian-li dropped on to his knees and covered my mouth in mid-scream with his hand. I bit it. Muttering a Chinese oath, he used both hands to press my chin and the top of my head together and continued to hold me in that vice while he went on talking.

Tilda also had screamed, he told me when the car had passed by. He had to stop her screaming. In the struggle which followed they had toppled together off a small bridge to which the little-used path had brought them. I knew already that it was a bridge over a sluice cutting, not over the canal itself, so I was not surprised to hear that the water was not too deep. Jian-li himself had landed on his feet, and the water came only up to his knees. But Tilda had fallen more awkwardly. She had hit her head and drowned. It was not his fault.

I didn't believe him. If half of that were the truth, he could easily have pulled her out. It seemed all too likely that he had seen his chance to prevent her from exposing him and had taken it, pressing her down beneath the surface until she drowned. He had wanted to silence her, and had succeeded. But while a small part of my mind was listening and drawing conclusions, most of my attention was on more distant sounds.

Someone had just rung the front door bell. After Griselda's death I had had a strident outdoor bell fixed to the wall of the house, to be audible if I was taking a class in the garden. It might not have attracted my attention now, at such a distance from the house, had the sound of the car not alerted me; but because I was listening, I knew when it rang.

Fighting Jian-li's grip, I managed to jerk my head with

such a vigorous gesture that he allowed me to open my mouth.

"I told you. An appointment. He'll come to look for me. You'd better run for it." How convenient it was that my lies should have come true. I wondered who the caller was. Could it be Bodger who was about to save my life for a second time? No, it was too early for that. The police, perhaps, with more questions. Surely, surely Maggie and Mrs Butler would suggest that they should come and look for me in the wood. Please. Please.

They would have to be quick. Jian-li was already standing up again. He moved across to the branch which he had earlier propped up against the tree. While his eyes were off me I twisted the wire even faster than before and gasped with relief as it snapped at last.

I took care not to reveal that I was partly free as I turned my head to watch him. In any chase or struggle he was bound to be the winner. Instead, I tried to calculate how best to twist my body when the branch began to fall. It was thick and heavy, but not completely straight. Angles and protuberances would provide arches of safety. And even if I couldn't take advantage of one of these, I didn't believe that its fall would kill me, as long as I managed to protect my head with my shoulders in some way.

Probably Jian-li didn't expect it to, either. All he needed was the appearance of an accident to cover whatever other plan he had in mind. In every possible sense, I was not out of the wood yet.

But that was the moment when the cavalry arrived.

Chapter Sixteen

It was a distinctly miniature troop of cavalry. One small Pekinese, pumping its tiny legs across the rough ground and yapping fit to bust. I'd heard that pekes are brave little fighters, but this particular bout of barking had nothing aggressive about it. Coco was proud to have tracked me down, and wanted me to know that he was pleased to see me. I appreciated the gesture, but would have been happier if he had been a rottweiler.

Jian-li could hardly have been alarmed by the prospect of – at worst – a nip on the ankles. But the noise and the movement together were enough to distract his attention for just long enough for me to get myself organised. Leaving my arms outstretched, as though the wrists were still attached to the main section of wire, I twisted my body away and at the same time jack-knifed it, bringing my feet up to press with bent knees against the tree-trunk. Then I fixed my eyes on him, watching for the first ripple of movement.

There wasn't long to wait. Jian-li took a step forward and heaved at the thick branch which earlier he had propped up against its mother tree. As soon as it began to fall towards me, I pushed off from the trunk with both feet, straightening my legs and rolling round so that the tree itself protected me. There was a crash as twiggy side-branches hit the ground, followed by a second thud to suggest that the wood had bounced before settling. In the silence which followed I lay still for a few seconds, stunned not by any physical blow but by the strain of anticipating and escaping it.

But this was no time to hang around. I scrambled to my feet, preparing to run before Jian-li moved on to the second part of his plan. It seemed, however, that we were no longer alone in the wood.

"Coco! Coco! Where are you, Coco?"

It was Mrs Butler's voice I could hear – and more welcome even than that was the sound of footsteps crackling through the carpet of last year's fall of beech leaves. Not one set of footsteps, but two.

"Over here!" I yelled, and stepped forward just as Mrs Butler came into sight. Strolling beside her was Bodger. Oh, darling Bodger! Always in the right place at the right time.

Jian-li might have believed that he could deal with two women, but the sight of a fit young man must have tipped the balance. He hesitated only for a moment before beginning to run. Bodger, meanwhile, was hurrying towards me.

"I know I'm early," he said. "Couldn't keep away from you." He opened his arms to embrace me, and looked puzzled for a moment when I made no attempt to reciprocate. Then he caught sight of my hands. They were covered with blood from the cutting wire which still bound them together at the wrists. My fingers too were bleeding where I had had to grasp the wire to twist and snap it. "What the hell— ?"

"Jian-li. He killed Tilda. He's been doing his best to kill me as well." Naturally I had told Bodger about the murder of my friend.

For a few seconds longer Bodger stared at my bleeding hands. Then he turned away and began to run through the wood, following the direction that Jian-li had taken.

200

"No, Bodger!" I shouted. In terms of fitness the two men might be evenly matched, but if it came to a fight Jian-li would be able to draw on the extra strength of desperation. When Bodger took no notice, I began to run after him; but came to a halt after only a few paces. Under normal circumstances I can run fast and I can run almost for ever – although not both at the same time – but my tied wrists would destroy my balance, and even if I caught them up I would be a liability to Bodger rather than a help. Anxiously I returned to where Mrs Butler was standing.

"Oh, Miss Quilter, I'm glad I've found you," she said as though nothing out of the ordinary had been happening. "I'm afraid Coco won't be suitable for your aunt, after all. He appears to have bonded himself to you instead. Most unfortunate. When the front door bell rang and he realised that a visitor had arrived, it should have been your aunt he alerted, but instead he seemed to think that you were the one he ought to track down. Obviously, with any placement, we give the dog special training in how he should relate to his handler, but in a case like this, when you would always be on the same premises, I really think we would do better to start again with a different dog. I've explained all this to your aunt. We'll try not to keep her waiting any longer than necessary. Coco!"

She stopped babbling and looked at me in an uncertain manner. "Coco?"

I had beaten her to the answer by several seconds, remembering the sudden silence which descended after the falling of the branch. To be honest, I had more on my mind than Coco's fate, but I could see that to Mrs Butler it was the only thing that mattered. I needed her help, and clearly would not get it until her own trouble was resolved. Stepping forward to examine the fallen branch, I pointed my hands down towards the ground.

"Oh no! Poor little Coco!" Mrs Butler tried without success to move the branch, but it was far too heavy for her. It was easy to see that there was no urgency in the matter. There was no movement, no life in the single leg which was all that could be seen.

"I'm so sorry." What more was there to say? "I'll arrange to have the branch lifted, and we'll bury him in the wood here, if that's all right by you."

It wasn't all right at all. I could read the thoughts passing through her mind as, disturbed by the sudden small tragedy, she looked up at all the trees around as though calculating whether this was a suitable environment for one of her precious animals.

Although I was desperate to get my hands free, anxiety on Maggie's account made me give this conversation my full attention.

"This wasn't an ordinary accident," I told her. "Someone was trying to kill me. It was Coco's arrival, in fact – and yours – that saved my life. I am truly very sorry for what has happened. But I can promise you that any dog you leave with Maggie will be loved and well cared for. The wood is quite safe except in the very worst gales, and of course we'd keep the dog in the house then. I do hope very much that you won't deprive Maggie of the help she needs so badly just because of what has happened to Coco."

"No," said Mrs Butler unsmilingly. "No, of course not. I'll be in touch."

"Please, before you go . . ." I held my hands out towards her; not just to show that I had not been exaggerating, but so that she could untie the wire for me. Still shocked and upset by the death of the dog, she hardly seemed to register what she was seeing; but she untwisted the wire in as matter-of-fact a manner as though she was unravelling a piece of knitting.

"Thank you." There was no time for excessive politeness. I began to run.

By now Jian-li had a good start, but he had gone in the wrong direction. He was heading for the ring road, but when he came to the edge of the wood he would find himself confronted by a double barrier: barbed wire and a muddy stream. This was not impassable, but would certainly slow him up. Bodger, naturally, had followed the same route. I had the advantage of knowing where there was an easier access to the road.

I ran in a diagonal line: past the house, past the terrace and the tennis lawn and the walled garden and then down across an area of parkland. The road curved round to meet me as I climbed over a section of ranch fencing and jumped the stream where it narrowed into a culvert. Pushing my way through the hedge of brambles which lined the road, I stepped out on to the cycle track.

Jian-li was running towards me on the track, making for the roundabout and – no doubt – the pick-up point for the express coaches to London. Bodger, with a torn trouser leg flapping, was in pursuit, but did not appear to be gaining on him. Jian-li's running style was not that of an athlete; his head was down and his arms pumped in an ungainly fashion. But it was carrying him along at a good rate of knots. I positioned myself in the centre of the track and steadied my balance.

He swerved as he approached, as though conscious of an obstruction without having registered who it was. Then he recognised me. Without changing pace he turned off the cycle track and ran straight across the road to the central reservation.

Nobody on this stretch of the ring road drives at less than seventy, and the traffic comes practically non-stop. There is a subway near the roundabout for pedestrians, but fear of muggers makes it unpopular, so that every year someone is killed trying to cross the road – and those are people who have time to stop and consider whether a gap is long enough. If Jian-li looked at all, it was in the wrong direction. It was only luck which carried him safely to the centre of the dual carriageway. I didn't care what happened to him. What made me catch my breath was the sight of Bodger also sprinting across the road.

They were both lucky; both catching the same gap in the traffic. I let my breath out with a sigh of relief.

There was no immediate opportunity for me to join them. As I waited for my chance, whizzing cars and lorries briefly obstructed my ringside view of what happened next. The central reservation is very wide. Most of it is grassed, but in the centre is a thick hedge of shrubs and trees, planted to reduce dazzle and act as a shock absorber in case of accident. As Jian-li continued to run in the direction of the roundabout, looking for a break in the hedge, Bodger threw himself forward in a rugger tackle.

It was successful, bringing his quarry down. But Jian-li had not been brought up to play that particular game in the proper spirit. He rolled on to his back, punching and kicking at the same time. By the time Bodger staggered to his feet, holding his head, Jian-li had pushed his way through the hedge.

My chance had come to cross to the centre. I made the dash and opened my mouth to ask Bodger if he was all right, but before I could speak there was a screeching of brakes, followed almost at once by the impact of metal upon metal. And again. And again. More braking. And then, just for a few seconds, an uncanny silence from that hidden part of the road; a silence broken eventually by the slamming of car doors, shouting, a scream.

Bodger, dazed by the blow to his head, was not aware of any of this.

"I can't see," he said. "The bastard! He kicked me in the eye."

First aid begins at home. To judge by the shouting on the far side of the bushes, there were enough people on the spot to look after casualties there. I unwound the already stained handkerchief which I had tied round one wrist and nervously dabbed away the blood which covered Bodger's eyes. To my relief, it all seemed to be coming from a single deep cut on his eyebrow.

"Keep this pressed down firmly," I told him, "and stand absolutely still for a moment, till I come back."

I found the gap in the hedge through which Jian-li had pushed himself and went just far enough to give myself a view of the accident. There were half a dozen people milling around, apparently unhurt, and at least three more sitting on the grass verge, head in hands, obviously in shock. But I could see only one dead body; and that was not in any of the damaged cars. Shocked myself, I returned to Bodger's side and, realising that he could still not see clearly, led him to the edge of the grass.

"We're going to cross the road back," I told him. "We shall have to run. Trust me. When I say 'Now'." I gripped his hand and elbow firmly. "Now!"

Stumbling slightly as we reached the cycle track, Bodger brought me to a halt.

"I'm not going to let him get away with this. Just give me a minute to clear my head, and—"

"He's not going to get away with anything," I assured him. "But first things first. I ought to get to a telephone as fast as I can and alert the ambulance and police that there's been an accident. There aren't any phones on that road. If you stay here, I'll bring a car round—"

"No. I can manage. I thought for a moment that he'd kicked my eye out, but it seems to be only blood that's blinding me."

More slowly than we had run down, we made our way up the slope to The Millstone. While Maggie registered horror and rushed to produce the first aid box, I dialled 999 and reported an accident on the ring road. Choosing, like more exalted persons, to be economical with the truth, I declared myself unable to give details but repeated that I had heard the sounds of braking and crashing. As I had.

By the time I returned to the kitchen Maggie had already cleaned Bodger up and was applying disinfectant. Knowing that she couldn't hear, he was letting rip with yells of protest, which came to a shamefaced end when he caught sight of me.

"Not blind after all," he reassured me cheerfully.

"You ought to go to Casualty, though, and have this stitched or clipped or whatever they do nowadays. Otherwise you're liable to be scarred for life."

"A scar is just what I need to give the right impression of derring-do. And sitting for five or six hours in a hospital waiting room is not my idea of fun. Especially if I were to find myself sitting next to someone who's been hurt through my fault."

"It wasn't your fault. Keep still, then." The cut was long and deep, but I had the right kind of butterfly plaster to hand, and with Maggie's help was able to draw the cut edges neatly together before applying it.

Then it was my turn to be patched up. At first I laughed – half-hysterically – at the discovery that for the second time in a month my hands were being put practically out of action; this time made clumsy by the plasters round each thumb and index finger. With that thought came the memory – pushed out of my mind by the events on the ring road – that for the second time in a month someone had tried to kill me. I found myself shivering with cold and shock.

"Good thing we're both wearing the same delicate

perfume," laughed Bodger, helping himself to a drink of water. "Dettol No 5." Turning, he realised for the first time that I was in a bit of a state. "Kit, what is it?"

There hadn't been time earlier on to tell him either what I had learned about Tilda's murder or exactly what had happened in the wood. I filled in the details now.

"You certainly have the knack of arriving in my life at the right moment."

"Seems to me I need to stay closer all the time, to stop you getting into these scrapes. Kit, why didn't you tell the police all this when you reported the accident? You're letting him get away."

I shook my head.

"Jian-li isn't going anywhere. He's dead. Run over."

"Oh, my God!" It was Bodger's turn to show signs of shock. He sat down to face me across the kitchen table. "I never meant . . . I mean, I was only trying to catch him and hand him over to the police. I didn't mean to kill him."

"And you didn't. It was an accident."

"But the accident was my fault. If I hadn't chased him . . . Oh, my God!"

Maggie, hovering in the background, was clearly frustrated by her inability to understand what was going on, but there wasn't time to pause and spell it out. I wasn't going to have Bodger taking any sort of blame at all on himself.

"Listen to me, Bodger." I put myself in the teaching mode. "What killed Jian-li was guilt. He didn't *have* to run away. And at the moment when he was knocked down, you were practically knocked out. I was the one who was still on my feet, so if he was running from anyone, it was from me. The reason he died was because he'd committed a crime and was frightened of being caught."

And probably because he hadn't expected there to

207

be another stretch of road on the further side of the hedge; and perhaps because when he saw it, he looked in the wrong direction for the traffic; but those were minor details.

There were a lot of people, it seemed to me, who deserved more sympathy than a murderous young student who had been too proud and too ambitious to accept failure honestly. The driver of the car which had knocked him down might know in his heart that he had no chance to stop, but probably still felt sick in his stomach. Other drivers had lost their cars and had perhaps been hurt.

And Tilda was dead. In any debate on capital punishment I speak against it, but at this moment I realised how deep-rooted is the concept of a life for a life. It was as though Tilda's spirit had invaded my mind after she was killed, and only now could be laid to rest. I didn't feel any guilt about what had happened. Only a comforting sense of peace – and gratitude.

"You and Coco saved my life this afternoon, Bodger," I said, going round the table to hug him from behind with my plastered hands. "A knight in shining armour and his rather small charger. You've had a nasty bang on the head. I think you ought to lie down for an hour or two. And then I'll come and say 'Thank you' properly."

Chapter Seventeen

I thought I had seen the last of Mr Tanaka, but on the day after Jian-li's death I found him standing by the front door. It was a blazing hot day, and my free week was still in progress, so I was wearing very short shorts, with a bikini top when I heard the bell. Mr Tanaka, by contrast, was immaculately dressed in a cream linen suit with shirt, tie and gloves. Gloves! Well, it's nice to know that not everyone allows standards to slip. I invited him to sit in the garden, where he chose a chair shaded by the umbrella and slowly eased off the gloves, one finger at a time.

His arrival was unwelcome and I wished I was wearing something more formal to give me confidence. Had he, I wondered, learned by now about the deception which Mayuko and Hiromi had inflicted on him? He could hardly think that the original plan had anything to do with me, but there was no doubt that I had helped the real Mayuko, at the time of her return to Japan, to escape detection. If he saw this as a personal humiliation, he would have cause to be angry; and from the moment of our first meeting the feeling between us had been not exactly cold, but certainly lacking warmth. I could read no more in his placid face now than when he first came to The Millstone; and not knowing what to expect made me uneasy.

Still, it was ridiculous to be suspicious of everyone who came near me, even though I might have done well to be more wary of one or two people rather earlier than I had been.

He was not a diplomat for nothing. Sensing my distrust, he metaphorically put on his kid gloves again before handling me. His voice was less abrasive than at our earlier meetings as we exchanged preliminary small-talk.

There was no reason, I reminded myself, to think of him as an opponent. He had performed his duties meticulously and it was neither his fault nor – to start with – mine if he had been deceived. We had both been put in the same boat of suckers. The first thing I needed to find out was whether he had yet discovered that fact.

He, however, was starting from a different point. Observing the bandages round my wrists and the plasters across my thumbs and fingers, he expressed sympathy for my injuries and tried to find out what had been going on. It occurred to me in good time that the lucrative flow of Japanese students could quickly dry up if the embassy were to issue a warning about the dangers of living in The Millstone – or suggest that its organiser was liable to attempt suicide by slashing her wrists. I put to good use the talent for inventing fictional situations which I use to set up my role play. In other words, I fibbed. Well, anyone might try to move a heavy casserole dish without realising that it had only just that moment been taken off the hob. Yes, thank you very much: the burns are much better already.

Then it was time for him to come to the point of his visit. It didn't take long for me to realise that yes, he had indeed discovered the truth about Mayuko's deception. I wondered how. May had proved unable to keep her secret, yet it was surely in the family's interests that no one other than those already privy to the true facts should discover them. But there was no time to think about that, because Mr Tanaka was still on diplomatic duty, playing the parts of soft man and hard man alternately himself in order

210

to get what he wanted. It was time for the hard man's act now.

His mission was to make it clear that if I were ever to sneak about what had happened there would be consequences. I admired the way in which he didn't precisely spell them out, whilst giving the impression that he could destroy my reputation and therefore my livelihood with a flick of one of his well-manicured fingers.

Oh no you couldn't, I thought to myself; but managed to suppress my rising fury until he had finished. Not all of it was directed at him. I had given May my word, when I accepted her apology, that I would do nothing to wreck her future. She ought to have trusted me instead of sending in a bully. And there was no doubt that bullying was the name of his game. Almost smugly now he was reminding me that thanks to Mr Fergie's insistence that there should be no photographs, I would never be able to back up any claims I might make about the identity of the Japanese student who had in fact enrolled with me.

He paused, apparently expecting me to shrivel into a worm and crawl away. It was my turn now.

"You're out of luck, I'm afraid, Mr Tanaka." I made myself speak pleasantly, as though I were not seething. "It's true that Hiromi, pretending to be Mayuko, doesn't appear in any group photographs. But a regular part of my teaching method involves making a video of the students' role play sessions, so that I can play them back later and discuss mistakes or suggest improvements in their conversation. In the normal course of events I record over the previous group as soon as a new course begins." Up to that point I was speaking the truth. "But in this case, as soon as I realised the importance of the evidence, I naturally put it into safe keeping."

That last remark was the sort of invention which comes from reading detective stories, when the chance to destroy evidence all too often provides a motive for murder. Not that I expected Mr Tanaka suddenly to produce a gun or a ceremonial sword. But it was time he realised how much I resented being put under pressure to do what I had already voluntarily promised. At that moment, indeed, I was almost ready to break my promise.

"And do you intend to produce this – evidence, as you call it?"

It was the question of a man who has lost an argument, and I allowed my annoyance to disperse with a single outflow of breath.

"I gave May my promise to keep her secret. Without threats and without bribes. I am disappointed that she apparently trusts me so little that she has to send you here to harass me. In fact, I hope you will tell me now that you have been acting only on the instructions of her uncle, without her knowledge."

We were eyeball to eyeball, and the pause was a long one. It was Mr Tanaka who blinked first. He felt in his breast pocket and produced two envelopes, one of which he handed to me without speaking.

The envelope was unsealed and contained a bankers' draft for ten thousand pounds. I stared at it almost – but not quite – unbelievingly. After the threat, the bribe. I remembered that Rufus also had been bought off – and with more reason as far as he was concerned, since he was being asked to give up his job. In my case, the money presented itself as a lack of trust; and because I was hurt by this, I was in no mood to hand it back.

Mr Tanaka was waiting to see what I would do. I was thinking about The Millstone's leaking roof.

"Thank you," I said formally. "I am disappointed that Mayuko doesn't trust me to honour my promise to her. But since she doesn't, she will probably feel more secure in her future life to know that she has bought me off. I presume you would like a receipt."

"If you please." Mr Tanaka's tone was equally formal and he had a paper ready. No doubt he enjoyed the view into my bikini as I bent over to sign with clumsy plastered fingers.

Not knowing what my normal signature looked like, he had no reason to query today's shaky scrawl.

"And the video recording?" he asked.

I led the way inside, found the cassette and slotted it into the adaptor. After playing enough of it on the television screen to show him that it was the right one, I first of all rewound it and then deliberately recorded over the whole tape.

Mr Tanaka sat patiently through this process and then handed me the second of the two envelopes he had been holding. "From Mayuko," he said. Bending his head in a farewell bow which I had no difficulty in recognising as a gesture to an inferior, he left me alone.

For a moment, hurt by Mayuko's lack of trust, I was tempted to throw the letter away. But for someone as inquisitive as myself, that gesture was never really on. I tore open the envelope.

'Dear Miss Quilter,' wrote Mayuko in perfect European script.

'When I visited your house you promised, in great kindness, not to tell anyone that I did not attend your language course as had been arranged. I find that I myself, though, am unwilling to tell all the lies that this secret involves. So I have spoken the truth to my aunt and uncle. They are very angry, and anxious in case their plans for me have been spoiled.

Although my uncle hopes that my foolish behaviour will never be made public, he has spoken on

213

the telephone to our ambassador in London, because there could be difficulties if in the future he discovers that he was not told the truth. My uncle has also sent presents of money, from the trust fund which my grandfather has left for me, to Hiromi and to Mr Fergie, asking them to forget what has happened. When he told me that he would send such money also to you, I said at first that this was not necessary because, in spite of my bad behaviour to you, you had made a promise to me and I was sure that you would not break it. But then I thought, why should you not also receive a present? Because Hiromi and Mr Fergie knew the truth all the time, but lies were told to you.

So I hope, Miss Quilter, that you will accept this gift from the trust. Whatever my uncle may wish, I ask nothing of you, because you have already given more than I deserve.'

As I came to the end of the first page, I found myself smiling at the realisation that my instinctive liking for May was well justified. Even in apology she had a certain dignity. She had made it easy for me to accept her gift with pleasure instead of in a mood of sulky revenge. With any luck, the era of the blue plastic buckets would soon be drawing to a close.

I spent a moment wondering about Mr Tanaka's role in all this. Why had he not simply handed over the money and the letter together? It was difficult to see what he would have had to gain by provoking me into refusing the gift. I could only think that he had wished to make my acceptance into a humiliation.

I turned back to finish reading May's letter. On the second page her handwriting was not quite so neat. Perhaps to begin with she had made a first draft and copied it out like an exercise: now she was being spontaneous.

'Before I left England you reminded me that the death of my grandfather would make me rich. That is true. Although for three years my uncle is still a trustee of the capital fund, I shall have at once a good income to spend as I like. In the plane going home I thought about the other thing you said, that I could choose to be free if I wished. And I have decided that this is indeed my wish. To see other countries and make many friends and not to be always formal and watched by photographers. And so very soon I shall tell my aunt and uncle that I do not wish to proceed with the marriage which they have hoped for me.

Although I need never work to earn money, there is work I would like to do. I take great pleasure in beautiful fabrics, and I would like one day to design beautiful dresses, like those I bought in Paris. First I must be taught, and if I come to Europe for this, I hope that we may meet again. There will be many arguments with my uncle, I know, but now that my grandfather is dead, there is no one who can prevent me.

Hiromi has told me how valuable were her lessons with you. I wish very much that I had been the one to enjoy them, as was first intended. But I thank you for your kindness when I did not deserve it.'

Good for you, Mayuko! It seemed to me, as I set the letter down, that I had taught her rather more than how to say 'please'. I had better hope that Uncle Shin never learned whom he had to thank for his niece's rebellion.

For perhaps half an hour I sat without moving in a state of contentment, enjoying the the heat of the sun on my

215

skin. There were urgent things to be done, such as putting my windfall on deposit and whistling up roof-repairers to give estimates. But it was delightful to relax for the first time in a month.

The rest of the week passed in the enjoyment of inertia. Plenty of things happened, but they were all good.

People began to scramble around on the roof, scribbling down figures which were astronomical but no longer completely out of reach.

Mrs Butler, full of Christian forgiveness, brought round a wriggling mass of love and warmth who was seventy-five per cent Jack Russell and a hundred per cent anxious to be useful.

Bodger also arrived at The Millstone for another visit. The accident on the ring road had left him less bouncy than before, but even more solicitous – as though, in spite of his flirtations with danger, he had only just for the first time recognised that people do sometimes die. I knew that someone so young, with a career to carve for himself, was never going to become the love of my life, and so did he, but that didn't diminish our happiness together.

Meanwhile, Mum was summoned to an identity parade and picked out not only the thug but also the driver of the car which had picked her up from the Bristol hotel. I mentally awarded myself a medal for ensuring that the Hiromi kidnapping had come to a happy ending, since nobody else seemed likely to give me much credit.

My other effort at playing detective was not so satisfactorily resolved. The temptation to hold my tongue on the subject of Tilda's murder was very great – and I succumbed to it. After all, the police had already made it clear that my interference was not appreciated. Would they be prepared to believe that someone might kill simply to prevent a small forgery from being discovered? Would I be able to persuade them that on a single signature rested not just a student's honour but his career, place of work and marriage? The Thames Valley Police were not trained to understand the Chinese mentality.

Besides, to volunteer the truth would be to invite questions about why I had not already reported the attack on myself, and the confession. Last but not least, Bodger would be interviewed, and interrogation might revive the feeling of guilt which I hoped I had smoothed away.

And Jian-li was dead, out of reach of further punishment. To establish the truth had been necessary for my peace of mind, but there was nothing more to be gained by making it public, except the tidying away of a police file.

Once I had made the decision, I stuck to it. It was time to welcome a new intake of students, to start a new course. Bodger left; work resumed. I was back in all the old routines, as though nothing out of the ordinary had happened, but my conscience must have remained uneasy. When one of the students reported that a policeman was approaching the house, I felt as guilty as though I were about to be accused of a crime myself. Was suppressing evidence a serious offence?

But it turned out to be only Mort, timing his visit on this occasion for elevenses.

"Big match this afternoon," he said, reminding me that the football season had begun again, long before the cricket season had ended. He didn't need to spell out what that meant: traffic chaos before three and after five, and drunken fans being sick in the streets for the rest of the evening. I thanked him for the warning.

"And I've got the date of the inquest for you. You'll be wanted."

Stupid with shock, I could feel my jaw dropping. How had they managed to link me with Jian-li's death? It didn't occur to me that it could be anything else. That's what a guilty conscience does for you.

217

"Surely I don't have to be there?"

"Well, you did say that there'd be no need for your young Japanese lady to hang around in England, because you were the one who saw what happened."

With an effort I managed to conceal my relief. Of course! He was talking about the inquest on the rapist.

"I thought the inquest was only concerned with his death in police custody. That doesn't have anything to do with me."

"The coroner would specially like you to attend. You're going to get a commendation, Kit my love. For doing your duty as a citizen without thought of your own safety, and all that jazz. So put on your best bib and tucker. You never know, you might find yourself on telly in the evening."

"Gracious! My fifteen minutes of fame!"

"Seriously, though, you did a good job there, and everyone's pleased to have it cleared up. Not the sort of thing we expect as a rule in a place like Oxford: rape and murder."

I couldn't help laughing. As well as helping to foil an attempted rape and discovering who had killed my friend, in the past few weeks I had had to cope with kidnapping, impersonation and two murderous assaults. That was just one person's ration of excitement.

All of this made it hard for me to feel too worried about the possible rampaging of Oxford United's opponents on a summer Saturday afternoon, but it would have been unkind to say so and deprive Mort of his excuse for calling. I knew how much he appreciated his cups of tea and home-made cake in Maggie's kitchen.

"Thank you very much for the warning about the football fans, Mort. As you say, it's nice to know that apart from them, Oxford is its sleepy old self again."